The Gold Bluff Deception

Maralee Wofford

A White Hat Book Club Presentation

ALL RIGHTS RESERVED

No part of this book may be reproduced or transmitted in any form or by any means, electronic or mechanical, including photocopying, recording, or by any information storage and retrieval system, without permission in writing from the author, except in the case of brief quotations embodied in reviews.

Cover Art:
Janelle Boatright (JanelleBoatright.com)

http://mlcdesigns4you.weebly.com/

Publisher's Note:

This is a work of fiction. All names, characters, places, and events are the work of the author's imagination.

Any resemblance to real persons, places, or events is coincidental.

Solstice Publishing - www.solsticepublishing.com

Copyright 2014 Maralee Wofford

THE GOLD BLUFF DECEPTION

BY

Maralee Wofford

A White Hat Book Club Novel

Port Orford Public Library
P.O. Box 130
Port Orford, OR 97465

The Gold Bluff Deception

This book is a work of fiction. The names, characters, places and incidents in this book are taken directly, and only, from the author's imagination. Any resemblances of actual persons, (with the exception of the characters, Tom Wenton and Bill Johnson, who were inspired by two very special friends of the author), locations and/or events are entirely coincidental.

No part of this book may be reproduced, other than the using of short quotes for reviews. The meaning of "All Rights Reserved" in the case of this book refers to all types of media, including electronic, audio and paper print. No translation of this book shall be made nor distributed. This book may not be scanned for any purpose. All of these rights are claimed by the author, and may not be breached except by the written approval of the author.

Maralee Lowder may be contacted at
info@maraleelowder.com

DEDICATION

THE GOLD BLUFF DECEPTION is dedicated in loving memory to Bill Johnson and Tom Taylor. Both masters of the too tall tale.

And, to my daughter, Laura Pallatin. This book's existence dates back to a conversation we had where she mentioned having read about a group of real estate investors who built a town very much like Gold Bluff. After the town was complete, they realized it was missing one very important component...its own history. This oversight was quickly remedied when they got together and created a history suitable to the city they created.

Chapter One

If anyone happened to glance at the two old men who sat outside the Golf Bluff Mercantile, they could not have helped but notice the dual glimmers of mischief sparkling from their eyes. The mid-summer sun warmed their tired bones as they rested on the store's weathered bench while watching the comings and goings of their neighbors.

The store's screen door swung open, drawing two pairs of curious eyes.

"Hey, there, Sammy," one of the two men greeted the man who had just left the store.

"Morning, Tom, Uncle Billy."

"Morning, Sam. Did you hear about that rainbow trout I took out'a the river last week? A real record breaker, she was."

"Humph! Some record," his friend snorted. "That fish along with three others."

"Now…"

"Sorry, fellas, I'd love to stay for the argument, but I've got a ten o'clock appointment to interview a teacher for the new high school. She ought to be here any minute now—wouldn't want to keep her waiting

The two old men watched the tall, angular younger man amble across the road.

"That Sammy. I've always said he was about the nicest guy this town has to offer."

"Yep, I always set quite a store by him myself."

"Can't figure out why he never got married."

"Sammy, married? Now, why'd he want to go and do something stupid like that?"

Just as Tom found the perfect retort to his friend's comment a well-traveled, four door sedan pulled up to the curb and parked. A bemused expression filled both of their eyes as they heard the car's spring's groan as an overly endowed woman climbed out of the driver's seat.

Each man nodded to her in greeting as the woman climbed the three steps leading into the store. As the screened door closed behind her, they turned their attentions away from her and back to the empty street.

*****

Eden's gaze locked on the image in the mirror. The furrow between her brows deepened as she examined her reflection one feature at a time. There was nothing like a job interview to remind a person of their inadequacies. Knowing the impact of first impressions, she'd gone way beyond her usual grooming routine, hoping to strike the perfect balance between her usual casual look and the professional appearance she imagined her interviewer would be looking for.

She'd thought long and hard before applying eyeliner and mascara. She really didn't like wearing all that goop on her face, but after grimacing at herself in the mirror, she'd decided the job interview called for the whole works, applying both with a light hand. The final touch was a russet hued lip-gloss, which brought out the deeper tones of her strawberry blond hair. That was it; she'd done just about all she could do.

Here she was dressed in an outfit she would never wear on the job, made up to look like someone she wasn't. She'd do all the textbook interview stuff, sit prim and proper, smile with the correct amount of intensity, and answer all the interviewer's questions with just the right amount of self-assurance. Did she dare show she had a sense of humor? Would it be considered an asset or a liability?

All this anxiety for a job she didn't actually need. She had a perfectly good job, for pity's sake. Even had tenure! Why go through all this? Because she wanted this job like she hadn't wanted anything for a very long time—that was why.

A thrill of expectation washed over her as she lowered her gaze to the opened magazine she had placed on the vanity beside her makeup case. "Gold Bluff, California", the title of the article read, "A City That Lives Its History." The photographs accompanying the article said nearly as much as the text. Wooden sidewalks, a relic of a general store, a gold rush era cemetery, all told of a town frozen in time. It was a history buff's dream come true…*her* dream come true.

*****

Leaving the old men to their people watching, Sam glanced both ways before crossing the street. Not surprisingly, there were no vehicles coming from either direction. He had to smile at himself. What had he expected, gridlock? Having spent most of his life dealing with the everyday craziness of one city or another, his urban survival instincts were firmly entrenched.

He checked his watch as he stepped onto the wooden walk, noting that he still had a few minutes left before his appointment. The smile left his face as he thought about the ordeal he was soon to be put through. Damn, he hated interviews! No matter how many questions you asked, how in hell were you expected to know which person would be the best for the job? When you got right down to it, some people were good at interviews and lousy at the job, while others were terrible at interviews and wonderful employees. From where he sat, the whole process was nothing but a crap shoot. And he was the guy who had to run the game.

*****

When Eden had first seen the article in Today's American Scene she'd been hopelessly entranced. The writer described a town, founded in the wild days of California's gold rush, still virtually intact. Set in the far northern part of the state, Gold Bluff had somehow managed to maintain its historical integrity yet still provide a lively, productive home for its residents.

    Although she was intrigued by the article, several months had passed before she found the time to check the town out. When she'd first picked up the magazine the fall semester was just getting into full swing, a time too filled with lesson plans and paper grading to allow her to do the sort of research her curiosity demanded. Finally, during spring break, she'd gone on the web, hoping to find more information about this unique city.

    The site was lovely, with photos echoing those she'd already seen in the Today's American Scene magazine along with text describing the local businesses and community happenings. She tapped at the link to the Gold Bluff Chamber of Commerce, spending nearly an hour checking out various business establishments. Returning to the main page, her attention was drawn to a link titled "Gold Bluff Unified School District – Employment Opportunities." Thinking, 'why not?' she clicked on it.

    It wasn't as if she was thinking of leaving her current job. She'd been teaching at the same high school in San Francisco ever since leaving college, and had no plans to leave. But still, it wouldn't hurt to look, right?

    Before turning off her computer she'd done far more than just look. From the moment the School District page opened she had been completely mesmerized. The high school was brand new and the School Board was in the process of accepting applications. A brand new school—away from the city—in an honest to goodness gold rush era town, could anything come closer to heaven?

    She wondered what else beside the high school was modern about Gold Bluff. From the pictures she had seen of the city it appeared as if the town had not changed since the days of California's famous gold rush. But, of course, that could hardly be possible. There must be some modern enterprises in or near the town. She just hoped there wouldn't be enough to spoil the town's charm.

Heart racing, she had filled out the online application, then sent it off into cyber space before stopping to wonder what she'd do if she was actually offered a position. Laughing at her uncharacteristically spontaneous action, she'd shut down the computer and put the whole incident out of her mind. She'd never hear back from them, so why worry?

But she had heard back. Phone calls had followed emails. An appointment had been made. And now here she was, staying in an honest-to-goodness boarding house, in an honest-to-goodness gold rush town, worrying about what to wear to an interview she had never believed would happen.

"Okay, kid, here you go!" she said as she closed the door to her room and descended the stairs. "Wish me luck, Mrs. Manning!" she called out to the boarding house's proprietor as she strode through the main gathering room.

"Oh, I do, dear. But you won't need luck from me. That job has your name written on it."

Eden wished she had as much confidence in herself as Mrs. Manning apparently did. Taking a deep breath, she squared her shoulders and began the short walk to the head of the School Board's office, leaving her car where she had parked it the previous night.

*****

"Morning, Sara," Bill Johnson greeted the middle aged woman as she walked up the steps of the store. "How are those two grandkids of yours?"

"They're doing fine, Uncle Billy. And you?"

"Couldn't be better."

He waited until the door closed firmly behind the woman before turning to his companion.

"A couple of heathens, those two," he said, his smile indicating that, in his opinion, being a heathen was a worthy accomplishment for a boy.

"Yeah, real wild Indians," Tom agreed with a sage nod.

Silence settled between them as they continued their vigil of the town's main street. A puff of warm, dry air swept down the street, past the two old men, pushing a swirl of dry leaves before it. The scent it carried promised that autumn would soon be upon the small mountain community.

The sound of a door opening and closing at Clara Manning's boarding house style bed and breakfast a few doors down the street caught both men's attention. They watched with interest as a young woman crossed the covered porch and stepped down the wide steps, then turned to walk in their direction.

"I bet that's her, that school teacher Sammy'll be interviewing. Kind'a small, but nice looking all the same." Uncle Billy's sky blue eyes lit up with interest as he tracked the young woman's progress. He watched appreciatively as she walked toward them.

"Too short. I like 'em leggier." Old Tom observed. His dry voice matched his looks, tall and lanky with the weathered skin of a man who had spent most of his days out of doors.

"Leggier! What's wrong with your eyes, old man? There's not a damn thing wrong with that girl's legs."

"That about four or five more inches wouldn't cure."

"And that comment comes from a man who picked a gal not more'n five feet tall to marry more'n fifty years ago. Your tastes change since then?"

"Nope, always liked 'em tall. Ella was just the exception, that's all. I married her in *spite* of her being just a tiny thing, not because of it."

"And I suppose you'd take points off for that girl's strawberry blond hair, which in my opinion is as pretty a sight as you're likely to see."

"Gives her freckles. Never could abide freckles."

"Freckles! Are you crazy, you doddering old fool? Why that young lady is …why, she's…" For once words completely abandoned Billy.

"Go on, you were saying?" Tom goaded.

"Nothin'. I wasn't saying nothin'," Uncle Billy harrumphed as he leaned back against the wall of the Gold Bluff Mercantile.

"He won't like her."

"What? Now that's just about the meanest thing you've said all day! What the heck's not to like about that nice young lady?"

"Heard she was from Frisco. Who wants someone who's been teaching those artsy fartsy kids down there?"

"Dang it! There you go again, saying the stupidest things just to get my goat!"

"Worked, didn't it?" When Tom chuckled his weather beaten old face formed a myriad of laugh wrinkles.

*****

Eden enjoyed the hollow sound her mid-heel pumps made as she walked along the wooden sidewalk. Far different from the sound her shoes made on the cement sidewalks she was accustomed to traversing. It gave her the sensation of having stepped backward in time by at least a hundred years.

Wooden sidewalks, for heaven's sake! And not just in front of one or two stores. From what she'd seen since arriving in town the night before, the entire town of Gold Bluff had them. Along with the most well preserved old buildings she'd ever seen. She couldn't imagine how the town could be more different from the Bay Area cities she had grown up in.

Maybe I should have worn the flower print dress, she worried to herself as she traveled the short distance from the bed-and-breakfast to the head of the School Board's office. Although it would never have been an option in San Francisco, here in the mountains she suspected it would have been a better choice.

She glanced down at her watch. Darn it. Not enough time to go back and change. Double darn!

A frown creased her brow as she checked the address on the building she was approaching against the one on the business card she held in her hand, verifying that yes indeed, it was the correct address. The address appeared to be correct, but the business sign in front of the building was not at all what she had expected. Gold Bluff Realty, it read in ornate Victorian style lettering.

She hesitated a moment, gazing at the sign. Her frown deepened. Damn, she hated real estate salesmen. After watching an old friend being tricked out of her home, she'd vowed to never have dealings with another slimy realtor for the rest of her life. Up until this moment it had been a vow she had kept quite easily.

The fluttering of a curtain and a quick movement at the window suggested she'd already been spotted by someone inside. The idea she was being watched really set her nerves on edge. She felt herself bristle at the thought it might be the man she had come to town to interview with. Watching her from behind a curtain seemed so damned sneaky. Something a real estate salesman would do.

That thought was definitely unsettling. Couldn't the guy give her the courtesy of letting her come face to face with him before he began drawing his opinions of her? That would be just like someone in his profession.

Of course, it might not be him. It could be one of the town gossips sneaking a quick peek at the teaching applicant. Although she'd spent her life living in the huge San Francisco metropolitan area, she'd heard enough about small towns to expect the gossip mills in Gold Bluff to be very active.

How many times had she been warned that if she moved to such a tiny town "everyone would know her business?" Her response had always been that when you lived as dull a life as she did, you didn't have to worry about town gossips. Heck, she kind of wished she had something interesting enough going on in her life to spark a little attention from time to time.

A thrill of excitement mixed with trepidation raced through her as she mounted the steps to her interviewer's office building. Ever since she'd arrived in town she'd felt as if she'd stepped back in time. That sensation completely enveloped her as she entered the beautifully maintained Victorian structure, pushing aside, at least for the moment, the unpleasant thoughts she'd allowed to creep into her mind.

The building was furnished to fit the needs of a working office while still retaining the atmosphere of the era in which it had been built. A Victorian era sofa, covered in deep burgundy brocade, flanked by a pair of leather chairs, faced an ornate fireplace. The secretary's work station, a large, heavily carved desk covered liberally with papers, framed photos and various office supplies, was near the window that looked out on Main Street.

On one corner of the huge desk sat a lovely vase of roses, which leant their soft aroma to the warmth of the setting. Scattered about the room were various antiques correct to the era of the building. The one noticeable exception to the vintage decor was the very up-to-date computer, which sat on its own stand to the side of the desk. If she had any doubts about the general atmosphere of the town, all she would have to do would be to look around this room and she would be quickly set right.

"Ah! Miss McKenna!" A sweet faced, middle-aged woman greeted Eden as she stepped through the door to the real estate office. "I'm Betty, Mr. Gorton's secretary. I saw you coming up the walkway there, and I said to myself, why, that must be our new little teacher. Dressed just like a 'school marm', in your lovely suit and all."

Eden winced at the phrase, "school marm." Although she *was* a teacher, and proud of it, she'd never thought of herself in exactly that term. But then, she'd never taught in an environment like Gold Bluff, California either, she reminded herself. In this town the term would probably be quite fitting.

Eden felt the heat move up her face. Yep, she definitely should have worn the flowered dress.

"I thought about changing into something a bit less severe, but if I had I would have been late for my appointment."

"You look just lovely, dear. It's just that we don't usually follow a strict dress code up here in Gold Bluff. But don't you worry about it a bit. Once you get to know us, you'll find the folks around here are more concerned about the sort of person you are, than about what you wear. You'll see we're all just one big family."

"That sounds absolutely wonderful. It's a far cry from the big city where you often don't know your next door neighbor's name."

"Oh, don't I know about that! I came from the city myself, not more than a year ago. And believe me when I tell you, I don't miss the hustle and bustle one bit. Not one bit!"

Eden decided that if Betty's beaming smile was as genuine as it appeared, living in Gold Bluff might be the experience she was hoping for. Just then the door to the left of Betty's desk opened. Tall, well over six feet, with a shock of dark brown hair, the bluest eyes Eden had ever seen, and a square jaw that might have been carved out of stone, his looks reminded her immediately of the Superman comic books her brother used to collect. "Wow", was the word that came to her mind as she stood gaping up at him.

"Miss McKenna? Eden McKenna?" he asked, his right brow lifting quizzically as he reached out to shake her hand.

She started to reach out to shake his hand, but drew it back suddenly when she realized she was holding her purse in her right hand.

"Oh! Yes! I'm here for an interview with the head of the School Board?"

"Who just happens to be me."

As if she wasn't embarrassed enough, she felt a swift flow of heat rise to her face. There was no way Mr. Gorton could possibly avoid seeing her monumental blush.

He smiled engagingly as he stepped aside to allow her to enter his office. "Head of the School Board, mayor, real estate broker, and head janitor just about covers it all," he continued as he gestured for her to take a seat in one of the chairs facing his desk.

It was even worse than she had thought. Her prospective boss wasn't just a real estate salesman he was a fully-fledged broker to boot! Could it get any worse?

Not only did this man represent an entire industry she considered to be evil incarnate, he had to be the handsomest man she had ever met—a man who could melt even the hardest heart with just his smile.

Great first impression, Eden groaned inwardly as she sank into the chair he indicated. *A little more babbling on my part and I might as well leave town right now.*

Looking at him across the desk, their eyes nearly level, he appeared far less intimidating than he had when he'd towered over her. Still, his masculine presence was enough to fill the room with a heavy dose of testosterone. In the past, testosterone had never had much of an effect on Eden. But, my-oh-my, it was working magic on her now!

*****

Sam could barely believe his eyes. Never in his wildest dreams would he have envisioned this beautiful creature as being a prospective employee. When had they started making high school teachers that looked like this? He hadn't been able to resist the temptation of drawing in a deep lungful of Eden's spring fresh scent as she had passed him on her way into his office. Was it his imagination, or had he felt a jolt of electricity when she came within inches of him?

Unfortunately, after seeing the stricken expression in her eyes when she'd first seen him, he felt fairly certain the attraction he felt for her was not likely to be reciprocated

"I've been looking forward to meeting you," he said, trying hard to control his voice .Eden settled herself into the chair, smoothing her skirt over her knees then looked up at him with a wary smile on her lips. He was gratified that she seemed to be relaxing a bit. He didn't know what it was about him that had caused her first reaction, but whatever it was he could only hope they would quickly get past it.

"I've read your resume with interest, Ms. McKenna, and I must say you're more than qualified for the position. Are you sure you'd want to leave the big city for a job in our little school? I see you have tenure in your present position."

"I work in a learning mill, Mr. Gorton. In at eight a.m., shuffle hundreds of kids in and out of my classroom every day, try to stuff a little knowledge down their throats and make it to the last bell without having to break up a fight between two or more of my students who are more interested in the latest antics of their favorite rap artists than they are about getting an education. The constant hassle of working in overcrowded classes, in a school so large it's impossible to remember the names of my students from one year to the next, plus the lack of time for truly creative teaching is not what I had in mind when I chose teaching as a profession. I'm hoping a smaller school will offer me an opportunity to really make a difference."

Sea green, that was the color of her eyes, he finally decided, the shifting green of a Caribbean lagoon.

"No, Mr. Gorton, I don't think I'll miss my old job very much at all."

Get your mind back where it belongs, he silently reprimanded himself. If he wasn't careful he could very easily make a huge fool of himself with this woman. He flashed her a smile, hoping it didn't come off as too wolfish. Giving himself a mental shake, he forced his mind back to the mundane questions he'd prepared.

"I see you double majored in English literature and American history, which is one of the reasons the board is interested in you. We're small time out here. Heck, when we open the doors to the new high school we'll have less than a couple hundred kids. Our teachers will all need to be qualified to teach at least two subjects. Your experience with both history and English fits in perfectly with our needs."

"And mine. The two subjects can be blended together beautifully. I'd like to see my students learn their history by writing essays and short stories about memorable characters from the past. We could even have them write a play featuring local history."

He felt his smile falter at her last statement.

"To tell you the truth, it was this town's unique history that piqued my interest in Gold Bluff in the first place. *Today's American Scene* is one of my favorite magazines, and when I read their wonderful article about this town, why I simply had to come here and see for myself where the Wenton family weathered their first winter. I can hardly wait to get out to their original homestead and see the very spot where Mrs. Wenton gave birth to triplets all alone during that terrible blizzard."

Now she really had his attention.

"Ah… yes, we do have an interesting past here in Gold Bluff, something to be proud of." He fought off the need to squirm in his chair, forcing himself to sit perfectly still. He was overreacting. *Keep your cool,* he reprimanded himself. *You can handle this.*

"Proud! I'd say so! This city's founders are what the very fabric of our country is based upon. Determined, hearty, brave. And you can't ignore their loyalty. How could anyone forget the story of how Daniel Wenton sacrificed his own life protecting those innocent Native Americans? But then, I don't suppose he realized he was going to die doing it. But that doesn't really matter, does it? What matters is he laid his life on the line for his Indian friends without thought to his own safety

He felt his heart sink as he listened to the enthusiasm in her retelling of Gold Bluff's "history." History was her passion and Gold Bluff was simply rife with it, right? Of course she'd be excited to find herself smack dab in the middle of such a colorful past.

"And then there was poor Abigail Wenton, left to raise those nine children all by herself. Along with the help she got from the grateful Indian tribe, of course."

"Of course." He pushed the two words through a throat tight with tension. "Abigail Wenton was one heck of a woman."

Chapter Two

"I tell ya, fellas, we've got to do something about this history thing. It's gotten way out of hand." Sam addressed the group of men who were sitting around the table in the back room of the High Trails Café—the same group of men who had been with him in this venture from the very beginning.

Joe Stanton, Sam's partner and friend of many years, groaned aloud. "Sammy, Sammy, Sammy. We've gone over this before. The history is what it is. There's no changing it now."

Murmurs of assent spread around the table.

"Mary, honey, can you bring us a couple fresh pitchers of beer back here?" Sammy called through the connecting door into the main room of the café. He was going to talk some sense into these guys if it took all night. And it never hurt to soften them up with a bit of ale. "And a platter of sandwiches," he added.

"Look, guys, when we started all this it was a joke. We built a town and then, just joking around, we 'built' its history. None of us meant for it to be taken seriously."

"And it wouldn't have been, if it hadn't been for those two old outlaws, Bill Johnson and Tom Wenton. It was all their doing, talking to that *Today's American Scene* lady like they did. I still don't know what those two were thinking of that day," George Bryant, the town's banker, grumbled.

"They were thinking the same thing they're always thinking—how to get themselves into more mischief," Joe offered. "As I recall, it was those two who supplied most of the details of Gold Bluff's 'past' in the first place."

"Well, we've all got to take a little blame there," Mason Bloomington spoke up for the first time. "We were all there when we started playing with the idea of making up a history for our little venture here. And, as I recall, we all contributed."

"But it was supposed to be a joke! Heck, Mason, when you printed up the flier with those outlandish lies, you never expected anyone to take it seriously, did you?" Sam answered.

"Of course not! I had every intention in the world of putting a disclaimer at the bottom of the flier that went into the promotion material. 'The above 'facts' are nothing but a pile of lies meant to entertain and amuse the reader,' was the exact wording of it. But, I guess I was distracted or something, and forgot to add that last bit before I sent it off to the printers.

"Then, when we noticed it wasn't there we'd already sold more than half of the property. Since none of the buyers had said the historical stuff had been a deciding point for choosing to move to Golf Bluff, we just figured what the hell, and never bothered to correct my mistake. How was I to know someone with a twisted sense of humor would give a flier to a writer for one of the most prestigious magazines on the stands?"

"It's all your fault, Sammy. If you hadn't gone along with Tom Wenton's idea of using his photos of old buildings from around here when we built the place, he wouldn't feel as if he owned the whole darned town."

"I know, Joe, believe me I know. I've heard the 'I told you so' routine every time that old reprobate gets himself into trouble. But none of that matters now. What matters is how we're going to stop this craziness."

"If only we'd known that writer was in town that day. We could have stopped this nonsense before it got so far out of hand," George shook his head soberly, bringing the subject back where it belonged.

"Yeah, and your bank would still have one teller, namely you, 'cuz you wouldn't have had enough customers to make it necessary to hire anyone else, much less the five people you have working for you now," Joe reminded him.

"And you, Sam, are you complaining about the landslide real estate business we've been doing ever sense that article came out? Mason, maybe you and George are unhappy with how well your investments in the venture have done. Is the fact that they've nearly quadrupled our investment been keeping the two of you awake nights?"

"Right, right, right. None of us planned for this to happen, it just did. And, to be fair, I've got to admit we've all profited from it. But what the heck do we do now? Continue perpetrating a lie?"

"That's exactly right, Sammy, old chum. Nothing changes. Not now, not ever," Mason interjected.

"What's so wrong, Sam?" George asked. "The town we built is exactly what it was meant to be—a place where people can come to live the life they've always dreamed of. A place where they can raise their kids that's got clean air, pure water, and the beauties of nature right outside their doors. It's the sort of town most people only dream about."

"Actually, the history aspect was not entirely made up," Mason interrupted. "There is the old Stossard mansion out there on the outskirts of town. That place has been here from the beginning. Heck, it must have been built back in the eighteen hundreds, which goes to prove there really was a town here at some time or other—a real town with a real history."

"That's right, Sam. So, since there really was a town here, it seems only right that we should have given it a history of its own."

"Only the history we're touting isn't the *real* history!" he practically shouted.

"But who *cares*?" Tom joined into the conversation, the strength of his voice equaling Sam's. "If anyone actually bought property here solely because of the history of the place they'd have to be out of their minds. This town is a success because of what we made of it, not because of what it once was."

As boys, Sam and Joe's parents had often brought them to camp in the shade of the now famous Gold Bluffs. They'd fished the nearby streams, climbed the bluffs, wandered through lush meadows. Neither of them had forgotten the endless hours they'd spent exploring the decrepit old buildings they'd found in a nearby valley.

Their imaginations were fired by the abandoned structures. Who had lived in them? Had it been a cattle ranch? Was that old building where real cowboys once slept? Why had the people left? Could they have all been killed in an Indian attack? Yeah! That was it, Indians!

One day, while the two families were enjoying their vacations, two old men happened onto their campsite. They introduced themselves as Tom Wenton and Bill Johnson. The two had been fishing the area for so long they knew all the best spots to catch the prized rainbow trout.

A friendship quickly blossomed between the old men and the two families, one that continued for many years. The two boys were particularly fascinated by the old men's expertise with their fly rods, and with Uncle Billy's incredible accuracy when it came to spitting tobacco juice.

By the time the boys reached high school their families had drifted apart when Sam's father changed jobs, forcing them to move to another state. It wasn't until Sam's new job brought him back to the San Francisco Bay Area and he looked Joe up that the thought of returning to their old vacation haunt was brought up again.

The night this current venture began the two men had been at Joe's house sharing a bottle of Jack Daniels while they soaked in a hot tub. It was a clear night which was a bit unusual for Sausalito, a city across the bay from San Francisco. The stars were so bright they reminded Sam of diamonds. Since Joe's wife and two daughters were off on a Girl Scout camping trip, he'd taken advantage of the situation by asking his old friend over for a game of golf, followed by barbequed steaks and a soothing soak.

"Look at those stars," Sam remarked as he took a sip of his drink. He laid his head back against the edge of the tub, cushioning it for a good long gaze at the heavens. "Kind of reminds me of all those times we went camping at Gold Bluff. Ah, those were great times, weren't they?"

"The best."

"Yeah," Joe sighed as he let himself sink a little deeper into the churning hot water. "You ever take Brenda and the girls up there? I bet the kids would love it just like we did."

"Always meant to. Never got around to it though. Too busy, I guess."

"Ah, come on, too busy to take your family on a vacation?"

"You can't believe how hectic my job gets. With business the way it's been lately, I'm lucky to get the odd Sunday off, much less an entire week. My boss would have a heart attack if I asked for more than a couple of days off."

"That sucks, man. How can you live like that? Here you have a wife most men only dream about and two of the cutest kids I've ever seen and you can't even take them on a vacation."

"Yeah, it sucks, all right. I just wish I could do something about it."

"You've *got* to, man! Come on, Joey old boy, why don't you call your boss right now and tell him you're taking a week off."

"Are you kidding? Old man Gruber would probably fire me on the spot if I did a thing like that. Nobody bothers him after hours, not if they're sane, that is."

"Ah, hell, he's not going to fire you. If he keeps you as busy as all that he must rely on you a whole heck of a lot. How long have you been working for him, anyway?"

"Nearly five years."

Joe thought for a minute of what he'd just said, then sat up a little straighter.

"Five freakin' years. Damn! I can't believe I've actually let that old fart coerce me into working all those years without taking more than three days off in a row."

"Call him. Tell him you're taking off for a week if it torques the whole damned company. Tell him if he doesn't like it you'll go to work for his biggest rival. Tell him…"

"Want to go camping?" Joe interrupted.

"Hell yes, I want to go camping! When do we go?"

"I'll get back to you on that." Joe replied as he let himself sink back into the hot foaming water.

*****

Sam figured Joe had lost his nerve. After all, if a guy could let his boss bully him into passing up vacations for five years, one night of being goaded into rebelling by a friend he hadn't seen in years wasn't likely to force him to stand up for his rights.

But Sammy was wrong. Joe made the call the very next day, and in less than three weeks Joe, his wife, Brenda, their two daughters and Sam, were all on their way to Gold Bluff, camping gear stowed in the rear of Brenda's trusty Ford Windstar.

As they drove north on Interstate Five, the men reminisced together about the wonderful vacations they'd shared as boys.

"Remember those two old men, Tom and Bill? Didn't we always call him Uncle Billy?" Joe asked Sam as he drove toward Mt. Shasta.

"Funny how, though we always seemed to run into those guys, we never did know where they lived. I always figured they had a cabin back up there somewhere in the woods. But, no matter how long we knew them, we never did see where it was."

"You don't think they'd still be up there, do you?" Sam asked.

"You know, they just might. They'd be older than sin by now, but, if I recall, Tom did say he owned a lot of land up there. If that's the case, they just might still be around."

"Wouldn't that be great? Wouldn't you love for your kids to meet those two?"

"Yeah, that would be super. All except for the spitting part, that is. I don't think Brenda would be too happy with that."

The vacation was a total success. Nothing about the area had changed. To the two men's great pleasure, they even discovered their old friends, Tom and Bill, were still impressing young fishermen with their very unique talents.

*****

"If you're so worried this new history teacher is going to scare up some trouble, don't hire her," George suggested. "She's not the only applicant for the position, is she?"

Not hire Eden McKenna simply because of her interest in history? No, that was a terrible reason for not hiring someone. Especially someone like Eden—he'd already started calling her by her given name in his mind, though not to her face, as that would have been far too forward at this point in time. No, Eden deserved better than to be rejected simply because of her passion for history. Such a passion should be respected—not rejected.

"I have interviewed a few other teachers but none of them come with her credentials—or with her experience. From what I've gathered she's a first rate teacher, both in English Lit *and* history. We'd be making a real mistake in not hiring her."

"But what if she starts digging around? Might cause us some real trouble," Joe worried.

"Think about it, Joe. This is the lady who will teach your own girls. Don't you want the best for them? I'm telling you, man, Eden McKenna is the best teacher we could ever hope to get for the money we're able to pay. We'll be damned lucky to get her."

"So you figure we should bite the bullet and go for it? Hope she's not so curious she'll dig where she shouldn't be digging?" Mason interjected in his raspy voice.

"Yeah," Sam replied. "We'll just all have to make sure to head her off if any of us see her looking where she shouldn't. We can do that, can't we?"

Chapter Three

With a final fluff to the white lace curtains at the living room window, Eden declared the job finished. The men from the moving company had left hours before, leaving her to transform her sparse collection of furniture and huge stack of boxes she'd brought from San Francisco into a home. Glancing around the small living room, she felt satisfied. Her belongings looked as if they'd been bought for this very house.

It wasn't as if she hadn't loved her home in the city—she had. But it had been so small! Carved out of an odd shaped corner of an old Victorian house, the L-shaped studio apartment barely held the period furniture she loved, much less the books that had become both her treasures and her nemesis.

Now, with all the room her new home gave her, she could collect books to her heart's content. She envisioned lining the living room walls with bookshelves, with her furniture placed comfortably about. She visualized it looking like a Victorian library.

To just about anyone else, the one bedroom Victorian house might have seemed a bit cramped, but to Eden it was a dream come true. The living room, though fairly moderate, by most people's standards, but huge to hers, opened onto a dining room of nearly equal proportions.

The built-in buffet in the dining room, rather than housing china, for which it had been designed, was now filled with rows of Eden's treasured books, as were the deep-set windowsills in both rooms.

The bedroom was her special delight. Years ago she'd rescued a badly tarnished, unbelievably ornate brass bed from the back room of a trash-to-treasure secondhand shop. Weeks of work had produced the gleaming treasure that was now the centerpiece of the room. Covered with a vintage hand crafted quilt, the bed was something to be proud of.

Totally wrapped up in the pleasure her new home gave her, she was suddenly startled by light tapping on the front door. Since she hadn't had a chance to make any friends since arriving that morning, her curiosity was piqued about who it could be as she went to open it.

When she opened the door she was greeted by a very odd sight. Two old men, one rather short and rotund, the other tall and lanky, stood on her porch. Each man was holding what appeared to be offerings.

"Good evening, Ma'am," the taller of the two spoke first, dipping his head in an abbreviated form of a bow. "Billy and I wanted to stop by to welcome you to town. Brought you a little something, just in case you hadn't had time to go shopping for your dinner."

"Hope you like fresh trout," the shorter man interjected. "Tom and I caught them just this morning, so's they're about as fresh as they need to be." The shorter of the two men awkwardly held the newspaper wrapped parcel toward her.

"And my wife, Ella, she baked up this blackberry cobbler for you—wanted you to get a taste of our own wild berries—thought they'd be a fittin' welcome to the new school marm."

"My goodness, how sweet! Won't you both please come in? I was just about to make myself a cup of tea. May I offer you both a cup?" She stepped aside, gesturing that both men should enter. "Why don't I put these in the refrigerator, then we can have ourselves a little visit," she suggested as she took the gifts from their outstretched hands.

After a brief jostling for position to determine which of the two men would step through the door first, they entered, Bill finally taking the lead. Tom took no more than two steps into the room before he stopped, an expression resembling awe settling upon his face. Without saying a word, he turned slowly around, his gaze taking in every detail of the room.

"Do you like what I've done with the place?" Eden asked, taken with the old man's apparent interest.

"Why, yes, very much," he replied. Although Tom responded quickly enough to Eden's question, his tone and manner gave her the impression he was barely aware of Billy's or her presence. His gaze settled first on one object then another. At the same time, a smile slowly crept over his face. When he finally turned to face Eden she noted a sparkling of tears shining in his eyes.

"I don't know how you did it, but you managed to fix this old house up just like Aunt Hattie had it. Yep, right down to the gilt mirror over the fireplace there. It's downright uncanny."

"You mean to tell me your very own aunt lived in this house?"

"'Till the day she died." He dipped his head with respect.

Billy made a sort of choking sound deep in his throat but kept his thoughts to himself.

"Why, I feel so honored! I hope you don't mind my living here."

"Mind! Why, I wouldn't have it any other way. My old aunt would love knowing the home she lived in for so many years was being graced by your lovely presence."

The noise Billy made at that statement was definitely a snort.

"What's the matter with you, old man? Getting so senile you forgot how to breathe?" Tom taunted.

"My memory's just fine, thank you. 'Course, it ain't as good as yours seems to be," Uncle Billy gave Tom a pointed look.

"It's all the reminders here in this room," Tom

glanced around the room once more. "It takes me back to my childhood, just being here."

"Better watch out, old man. That's a long trip you're taking there. Wouldn't want you getting lost."

"Why don't I get us that tea?" Eden suggested, deciding it might be a good idea to get the two old men interested in something else before their bantering had a chance to get really serious.

"Would it be okay if I took a look at the rest of the place? It's just amazing how much it looks like it did when Aunt Hat lived here."

"No, of course not. Please, let me show you the bedroom and bath."

She opened the bedroom door and stepped through, making way for both elderly gentlemen.

Tom stepped into the room far enough to allow Uncle Billy to enter, then stopped dead in his tracks. From his viewpoint he could see the entire room and into the bathroom.

"My goodness," he said, his voice echoing a sense of awe. "They left that old claw-foot tub. And I bet you have to pull a cord to flush the toilet, right?"

"Yes, I do!"

"Well, that's easily enough explained. Would have cost 'em money to upgrade, though most folks probably would have. But what's truly amazing is this bed. Why, I do declare it's just about an exact replica of the one my aunt had."

The sight of Eden's ornate bed seemed to bring old Tom's speech to a halt. He just stood there looking at it, taking in its intricate workmanship, the antique Grandmother's Flower Garden quilt covering it, and the hand embroidered pillowcases Eden had made herself. His eyes misted over until one tear slipped out, trailing slowly down his weather beaten cheek.

If Eden had been able to remove her astonished

gaze from Tom, she would have noted a vastly different expression on Bill Johnson's face.

"Kind a takes you back, huh?" he goaded his old friend.

Billy's words brought Eden's attention back to him. The emotions she saw on Billy's chubby, bristle-covered face were a mixture of amusement, disbelief, and pure and simple awe.

"Oh, my, yes. She was my favorite aunt, you know," Tom turned toward Billy, winking at him.

"Your Aunt Hattie? Why, yes! Of course I remember all the tales you used to tell me about her. I remember you telling me how she used to make you her famous gingerbread cake, and how she'd cover it with home churned ice cream."

"And she'd always serve it to me with a cup of steaming hot tea." Tom turned a baleful eye toward Eden, as if he were reminding her of her previous offer.

"Tea! Right, I forgot our tea, didn't I? Let me just put the kettle on and I'll have it ready in no time at all."

Eden smiled to herself as she left the room to prepare the promised tea. She wondered if her absence was even noted by the two old friends as she heard the sound of their voices continue.

"Your dear old Aunt Hattie?" Billy hissed under his breath after Eden left the room. "Now, why did you go on about your nonexistent aunt to that sweet little lady? You know you never had any such aunt."

"You may not know it, but I did so have an Aunt Hattie. As a matter of fact, I was her very favorite nephew."

"Humph! Right," was all Billy could manage to come up with at the moment. He really hated it when Tom got the better of him, and this was one of those times.

Eden had no more served the tea than there was another rapping at the door. Opening it, she was surprised to see Sam Gorton standing before her holding a huge bouquet of roses.

"Why, Mr. Gorton, what a lovely surprise! Won't you come in?" she asked as she stepped aside to let him pass. "I'm sure you already know Mr. Wenton and Mr. Johnson?"

She glanced at the two old men, both of them beaming up at her newest visitor with apparently unbridled pleasure. The picture of gentility, both men sat on the edge of their chairs, carefully balancing delicate cups and saucers on their knees. Turning back to Sam, she was rather shocked at the stern expression he was directing to her other guests.

"We're having some tea. May I get you a cup?"

"Please," Sam answered through clenched teeth. Bringing flowers as a welcoming gift for the new teacher had seemed a good idea. Now he saw it in an entirely different light. Rather than using them as a way of welcoming her, he now saw it as an opportunity to head off whatever mischief those two old reprobates were up to.

"And the flowers?" she asked, smiling at him with the sweetest of smiles.

"Are for you." Sam turned his gaze to her. As he looked into her teal green eyes, he forgot for a moment that two sets of old eyes were watching. The two old men were forgotten as he extended the bouquet.

"They're lovely, Mr. Gorton. Are they from your own garden?" she asked as she buried her face amongst the multicolored blooms. Yellow, lavender, pink and white roses exuded their sweet scent, filling the room with their aroma.

"Ah, no, they're from my neighbor's yard. She offered them when I mentioned to her that what Gold Bluff needed was a flower shop—that I wanted to buy you a welcoming bouquet."

"You must tell her how much I appreciate her thoughtfulness. Oh, and yours too, of course."

Until that moment, Sam had never been particularly charmed by a woman's blush. But then he'd never had the delightful experience of knowing he'd been the cause of one on such a lovely woman before.

"I will," he replied. He felt himself being drawn even deeper into the depths of her eyes. It was almost as if he was gazing into two emerald hued crystal balls that contained the secrets of life itself.

"Better get those roses in water before they start to wilt," Tom's dry voice broke into the charged silence.

"Of course!" Eden's smile changed from one of bliss to an embarrassed grin. "I'll just take these into the kitchen and look for a vase while I reheat the water for more tea. You did say you would have a cup of tea with us, didn't you Mr. Gorton?"

"I wouldn't miss it for the world." He gave the two men seated in matching velvet tufted chairs a meaningful stare as Eden left the room.

"What the heck are you two up to?" He whispered furiously.

"Who?"

"Us?"

"Why, we were just…"

"Thought we should welcome the new school marm, that's all."

"Seein' as I'm the only living member of this town's founding family we thought it only fitting…"

"Oh, don't give me that 'founding family' lie. You two can't just…"

"Lie! Now, hold on there, sunny. I'll have you know…"

"Ah, here we are. I forgot to ask you what you wanted in your tea, Mr. Gorton, so I brought everything I could think of. Sugar? Cream? Lemon?"

"I see you're all set up here," Sam glanced around the room appreciatively. "School won't be starting for another couple of weeks. Perhaps you'd like to do a little sightseeing before settling down to work. I'd love to show you some of our special attractions. Don't want you getting bored."

"Bored! Oh, Mr. Gorton, I could never get bored around here. Besides, I'll need most of that time to get my lesson plans in order. But, yes, I'd love to get out and see some of the sights. But most especially, I'd like to see the Wenton family homestead."

Sam felt his smile freeze when she mentioned the Wenton place. This was not going at all as he had hoped.

Turning to Tom, she continued, "Would I be presuming too much by asking you to come to the ranch with us, Tom? I can't think of anyone who would know more of its past than you."

"Of course we'll come along, won't we Billy?"

"Wouldn't miss it for the world," Bill replied with a smile. A mischievous gleam lit up his eyes at the same moment that Sam began coughing.

Eden turned back to Sam. Her pretty smile immediately changed to a look of concern.

"Mr. Gorton! Are you all right? Did your tea go down wrong?"

"I'm fine," he sputtered. "Just fine." He coughed a couple more times, all the while glaring at the two older men.

When he'd finally gotten over his coughing fit, Sam rose. "I hate to break up this party, but I bet Ms. McKenna's just about done in. Maybe the three of us ought to let her get some rest." He directed his last remarks very pointedly at Tom and Uncle Billy.

"But, I…" Apparently Tom was not at all ready to go. But Billy, being the true gentleman that he was, urged his friend to come along and let Eden eat the dinner they'd brought.

"We'll go out to the Wenton place, won't we?" Eden called out as the three men left.

"If that's what you want." Sam tried his darnedest to make his smile appear genuine. The anxiety he felt rising in his chest made an honest smile hard to come by.

"I don't want to put you out. That is, if you're too busy maybe it would be better if Tom and Bill showed it to me."

"No! I mean, no, I wouldn't think of it. In fact, I'm looking forward to it! I can't think of anything I'd rather do than show you Gold Bluff's founding family's original home. Why don't we plan on going tomorrow? Is tomorrow good for you guys?" He asked Tom and Billy.

"Fine with us," Tom replied, a grin creasing his weather beaten face.

"And you, Eden? Would tomorrow morning around ten work?"

"That would be lovely," she replied.

"Well fine then. That settles it, doesn't it?"

As she watched the men walk away, Eden couldn't help wondering what had come over Mr. Gorton. His words sounded as if he really wanted to take her to the Wenton ranch, but the look on his face sure didn't. If he didn't want to go, why didn't he just say so? She would have been perfectly happy to go there with just Tom and Bill.

Actually, that wasn't quite true. She really did like Sam Gorton's company in spite of him being one of those real estate people. Too bad he was her boss. If she'd learned one thing in life, it was that becoming personally involved with your employer was never a good idea. So, it didn't matter how much she might be taken in by his tall good looks or his utterly charming smile, the man was definitely off limits to her. Darn it, anyway!

Chapter Four

It was mid-morning the next day when the four of them headed out of town in Sam's white Ford Bronco. He had rolled the windows down to allow the fresh air to circulate freely

"Too much wind for you back there?" he called over his shoulder to the two older men who occupied the back seat.

"No, we can manage," Tom replied in a tone that suggested he wouldn't complain even if the wind reached gale force proportions.

"Never mind what he says," Billy countered. "Roll those things up. Soon as we get off this paved road and hit the dirt we'll be choking back here. What are you trying to do, kill us?"

Actually, the thought had flitted across Sam's mind a time or two in the last twenty-four hours. But he supposed death by fresh, dirt filled, air was not the most efficient manner in which to achieve that goal. He rolled the windows up to a more civilized position without making another comment.

Glancing over at Eden, Sam noted she appeared to be checking out each building they passed. He knew she'd had little time to see much of the town since moving there just the day before, so she must be more than a little curious.

He relaxed a bit. He was proud of the town, as well he should be. After all, he'd spent many hours and more money than he wanted to think about to help give it a hometown appearance.

The downtown area, composed of old, gold rush era buildings, was well kept and bustling with activity. No boarded-up empty store fronts marred their view as they drove slowly by. Town folk and a few tourists strolled the walkways, wandering into stores or glancing in the windows, passing the time of day with one another.

His heart swelled with pride. Yes, this was exactly what he'd dreamed it would be; America's hometown. And none of it would have happened if not for him and his partners.

"Oh, Mr. Gorton, isn't that the cutest thing you ever saw?" Eden gestured to a family standing outside the ice cream shop. Mother, father, and their two children all held ice cream cones and appeared to be enjoying them immensely. The smallest boy held a cone in one hand, to which he was giving all of his little-boy attention. His other hand was holding a second cone out to a huge Golden Retriever. The dog, nearly eye level to the little boy, lapped happily at his treat.

"Oh, that's the Pettigrew family. Great kids. And, as you can see, their dog's pretty great too. Ed Pettigrew, he's the town pharmacist. He must have stepped out of his shop for an ice cream break with the family."

"Hey, there, Ed," Sam had rolled his window down so he could call a greeting to the father. "Enjoying this weather?"

The entire Pettigrew family stopped slurping their ice cream long enough to wave a greeting to Sam and his passengers. All except the dog, that is. He was far too interested in his treat to stop even for an instant.

As they passed out of town, the older buildings began to give way to more modern, up-to-date models. Yet even these newer homes all possessed a sense of the era in which Gold Bluff had originally been created. White picket fencing was the norm here, along with broad lawns and old growth trees.

Soon they came to the baseball field and its adjacent parking lot. On the far side of the parking lot was the community swimming pool, which at this moment was filled with children and their parents. With school starting in little less than two weeks, most of the town's kids were intent on making the most of their last few days of freedom.

"I don't suppose you've had a chance to see Founder's Park yet?" Sam asked Eden.

"I haven't had time to see anything!"

"Well then, we'll have to make a little detour," he said as he turned the car onto a dirt road that led toward the river. "We're kind'a proud of our little park, right guys?"

"Would be if they'd named it Wenton Park like they should'a," Tom grumbled from the back seat. "If you're going to name something after the founders of a place, seems only reasonable you'd want to use the founders' name—which, in this case, happens to be 'Wenton'."

"Tom, if you had your way, everything in the valley would've been named Wenton this or Wenton that."

"Would've been alright with me," Tom answered cryptically.

Sam's only response was to look out his side window as he shook his head with frustration. Though he'd known the old man for most of his life he still found Tom's irascible attitude a bit much at times. The old guy just didn't get the picture!

There was so much more to this real estate venture than Tom seemed able to fathom. It wasn't just about the Wenton family's old homestead. It was about now, today, this very moment. It was about making Gold Bluff the financial success Sam and his partners had envisioned.

"Oh, Mr. Gorton, this is so beautiful!" Eden broke into his thoughts with her lilting voice. "What a wonderful spot for a picnic."

Eden's praise worked like a soothing balm on Sam. He loved the park, was inordinately proud to have been a part of its development. It had been his idea to build it here along the tree shaded banks of the river, among the wild rhododendron and blackberry bushes. He'd been the one who had pushed the partners to put in the children's playground and swing sets.

"How about forgetting the 'Mr. Gorton' thing? No one in Gold Bluff is all that formal. Everyone around here just calls me Sam."

Driving past a grouping of picnic tables, he pulled alongside the built up platform that served as a bandstand. He let the car idle while they watched the river flow by. A sandy beach ran along the river, which was wide and shallow at that point. It was a perfect place for toddlers to splash in the water under the watchful eyes of their parents.

"This is so wonderful," Eden sighed. "It's so... so...so last century!" She turned to smile at Sam.

"About as 'last century' as yesterday," Billy mumbled to his old buddy, in a voice barely loud enough to carry into the front seat.

"That's what I was thinking," Tom concurred in a voice clearly audible to everyone in the car.

"Uh, yeah," Sam cleared his throat as he put the car in reverse, turning it around to head on back to the road. "I thought you'd like to see the park, but we'd better get going if we want to spend much time at the Wenton homestead."

When they reached the paved road, Sam once again headed the car away from town, all the time wondering if there was some way he could permanently get rid of that old coot, Tom Wenton and his cohort, Billy, short of murder. But then, murder would do if nothing else came to mind.

They drove due east, the golden hued bluffs that had given the town its name rising majestically from the forest to their left. Every now and again Eden exclaimed in delight as she caught a glimpse of a river flowing off a steep decline to their right.

They'd traveled less than a mile when the paving ended. Soon it narrowed into a one lane dirt road used mainly by logging trucks. The forest seemed to close in around the car now, giving Eden the sensation that she and the men were the sole occupants of this vast tree filled expanse. It gave her a taste of what she suspected the pioneers must have felt when they'd first come to the region. Tall trees rose on both sides of the road, nearly blocking out the sun. She wondered how a horse drawn wagon could have traversed through the thick woods.

The car had been steadily climbing for nearly a mile when they finally reached the summit. The road turned toward the bluffs briefly, then reversed itself sharply at the crest. Sam pulled to a halt just as they reached the peak, allowing Eden an opportunity to savor the view below.

Nothing Eden had imagined could have prepared her for the sight before her. The valley below might have come from her dreams. Long and narrow, it consisted of over a mile of verdant green meadows, laced with wandering streams. High tree covered mountains rose from all sides, creating the sensation that she had discovered Shangri La.

Although most of the buildings were hidden by the forest a ranch had once stood at the nearest end of the valley. Her heart raced as she realized she was getting her very first glimpse of the Wenton homestead. And what a sight it was.

*****

As much as Eden was enjoying the view of the valley below, Sam was enjoying the sight of her. He marveled at how expressive her face was. From the glow he saw in her eyes he had no doubt she was completely entranced by the vista that spread out below them so magnificently.

He remembered the first time he'd seen this valley. He'd been twelve years old and it was a sight he'd carried with him the rest of his life. It was part of what had drawn him back to the region when he'd returned to California. And the preservation of this valley in its pristine state was the one thing he'd fought for when the investors began drawing up plans for the Gold Bluff development.

"Oh, Tom," Eden sighed. "How you must have loved living in such a wonderful place."

Tom cleared his throat, drawing Sam's attention. He glanced over his shoulder to the old man, groaning inwardly. Tom had reached for his handkerchief and was using it to wipe tears from his eyes. "Seeing it again does bring back a lot of memories," Tom replied in a choked voice. "A lot of 'em good, and few not so good."

"I just hope reviewing the glorious days of the past isn't too much for you, pal," Sam said dryly as he pointed the car down the steep road, taking them to the floor of the valley.

What an actor, Sam thought as he pulled the car to a halt in front of the deserted farmhouse. If he didn't know the truth, he'd believe the old coot himself. He just wished the old guy would give it a rest. As far as Sam was concerned the joke had gone on long enough. If Tom kept it up, he stood a good chance of messing up the very lucrative deal they all had going. Had he forgotten he stood to lose just as much as the rest of the investors?

Eden was out of the car before Sam had a chance to get out and open the door for her. By the rapt expression he saw on her face, he realized she was totally into the idea of exploring the old buildings.

"Is it okay if we go inside?" Eden called over her shoulder as she pushed open the sagging gate on the picket fence.

"You go right ahead," Tom told her. "My granddaddy built the place strong enough to withstand a tornado. 'Course, there weren't no tornados out here in California, so's it's as sound now as it was when he built it."

"What do you mean there's no tornados in California?" Billy protested. "Why, I remember one down in Long Beach when I was a boy that tore up…"

"I meant there weren't none here, you old fool. What do I care about what happened down in Long Beach!"

"Well, you did say 'in California', didn't you? You forgetting there's other parts to California? Heck, all the way up here, we might as well be in Oregon."

"But we aren't, are we?"

"That's enough!" Sam had just about had his fill of the two old men's bantering. He usually found them amusing, but they were really getting on his nerves today. If only he'd been able to bring Eden out here without the two of them.

"Who's coming in with me?" Eden called out as she stepped onto the porch.

"You go," Tom nodded his head toward Sam. "Billy and I'll stay out here, if it's all the same with you. The stairs are a little hard on our old joints, aren't they Billy?"

"That they are. And you know how going through his old home affects Tom. Gets him all teary eyed, remembering his boyhood days," Billy added, his face the perfect picture of innocence.

"You make sure she takes those stairs carefully," Tom cautioned Sam. "The third tread is a little wobbly."

"Yeah, right, the third step from the top," Billy added.

"And Eden, honey, just so's you know the layout, the back bedroom on your right was my brother Eldon's and mine. The big front one was my mother's and father's room."

The tour of the empty house took longer than Sam would have expected. But then, he'd never toured an abandoned old house with a history teacher before, he reminded himself as Eden checked out every nook and cranny. On his own, Sam had never given a thought to the construction of the stone fireplace, nor the uneven planking of the kitchen counters. He watched in fascination as she opened and closed each cabinet door, paying particular attention to the old hinges and the way the kitchen drawers still rolled out smoothly, though they had been constructed over a hundred years before.

They mounted the stairs to the upper story, with Sam dutifully reminding her to mind the third tread from the top, though he firmly doubted the need. Surely, that little bit of trivia about the old house was nothing but a figment of Tom's wily imagination, meant only to fool Eden into believing he had actually lived in the old place.

Perhaps in deference to Tom's "memories", Eden chose to explore the room he had described as his own when they first reached the second floor. Except for a few scraps of deteriorating wall paper, the room was completely bare. Eden walked to the window which faced the rear of the house, and glanced out of it.

Turning to Sam, she said, "It's so small. Hardly large enough for one boy, much less two, don't you think? But then, I suppose young people back then weren't used to the space today's kids expect. Heck, they probably had to share the same bed."

There were two more small bedrooms to explore, neither of them much larger than the first. The last bedroom they inspected was the largest, the room set aside for the owner and his wife.

"Oh, look!" Eden exclaimed as they stepped into the room. Tattered curtains still hung from the windows, masking views from three sides of the room. "This room is enormous!"

It was quite spacious considering the proportions of the rest of the house. Filling the entire south end of the building, its four large windows allowed it to be flooded with light. Sam sensed instinctively that the man who built the house meant for this room to be special, an expression of his love for the woman with whom he would share it.

"And look! Oh, I can't believe this," Eden

exclaimed as she spied a chest of drawers in the corner to their left. "With the rest of the house being completely empty, I'd never have expected to find something like this."

Her fingers trembling with excitement, Eden traced the carvings on each drawer. Glancing at Sam with the thrill of discovery shining in her eyes, she slowly opened one of the two top drawers. Once again, she reverently ran her fingers over the wood, as if by simply touching its surface she could experience its past. After a few moments she gently pushed the drawer closed, then opened its mate.

"There's something here," she said as she reached inside the drawer and pulled out a very old leather bound book. "Oh-my-gosh! It's a journal!"

"Who's journal?" *Damn! What the heck was going on now? No one had told him anything about any journal!*

Eden turned to him, an expression of curiosity in her eyes.

"I don't know whose journal it is," she replied as she reached out to hand the book to him. "Maybe we should ask Tom if it's his mother's. After all, this was her room, wasn't it?"

"So he says," Sam answered cryptically. He turned abruptly toward the door, his body language indicating that the house tour was now over.

*****

"Well, what do you think?" Eden asked Tom, her eyes sparkling with excitement. "Does the handwriting look familiar?"

"Oh, it's my mother's writing, all right. I'm just a little surprised she found the time to keep a diary. Must have done it at night after us kids went to bed, is all I can figure."

"Oh, Tom, isn't this wonderful? After all these years you can read about your mother's life in her very own words. Aren't you just thrilled?"

"I don't rightly know how I feel, to tell you the truth. This… well …" he had to stop to clear his throat, "I don't know as I'd feel right reading Mother's personal thoughts. I've carried her in my heart all these years, knowing her in my own special way. I'm thinking that reading this book might change things somehow."

He held the book out to Eden.

"No, I think I'd rather just leave things as they are. You take it. It's part of history and you're the history teacher, right? Maybe, after you're finished studying it and all, we can put it in the town's museum."

"Except, we don't have a museum," Sam interjected sourly.

"Which is a subject near to Tom's and my heart," said Uncle Billy. "We been saying all along that what Gold Bluff needs is its own museum."

"Of course it does! And this wonderful journal should have an honored place in it." Eden's eyes glowed with excitement. "As well as the chest it was left in, don't you think?" she turned to Sam, her expression indicating her confidence he would just naturally agree with her.

"Oh, right, mustn't forget the chest of drawers."

*****

"What the heck were you thinking?" Sam hissed to Tom. But rather than answer, the old man simply turned to look at Sam with one of his notorious innocent expressions.

Sam had let Billy and Eden take the lead as the group walked away from the house toward the barn and its connecting corral. He needed a little privacy with old Tom. If that old coot thought he was going to get away with his funny business, he was dead wrong!

"Oh, don't give me that innocent look. You've been up to your shenanigans again, but this time you're not getting away with it."

"I have no idea what you're talking about," Tom replied.

"No? Do you expect me to believe that piece of furniture got itself up those stairs and into that room all by itself? And that 'your mother's' journal just happened to be in it?"

"Son, sometimes miraculous things happen that can never be explained. I figure this is one of those times."

"Yeah, right, miraculous. And cows can fly."

"Never saw it, but who knows, maybe they can."

Sam chose to ignore Tom's last remark. "I'd like to know what you hope to gain by planting that fake journal."

"What makes you think it's fake?"

Sam cringed at the look of complete innocence on the old man's face. He knew from vast experience when Tom Wenton wore that expression trouble was just around the corner.

Chapter Five

The first day of school—a new job, a new town, a clean slate. Eden could barely contain her excitement as she stood before her students that morning. Barely more than a dozen of them sat before her, a far cry from her former experience. These students looked so fresh, so ready to learn.

"Good morning," she said, her smile radiating the excitement she could barely contain. "I hope you are all as excited as I am to be here."

She suppressed a grin as several of the students, all boys, groaned aloud.

"Okay, okay, maybe I'm being a bit over enthusiastic, but if you only knew the kind of school I'm used to working in, you would understand my enthusiasm."

"So, where are you from?" one of the boys sitting in the back row asked.

"I've been teaching high school in San Francisco for the past eleven years. And, though some of you may long for the excitement of the big city, I'm here to tell you, you are extremely fortunate to be able to attend school here, in this wonderful area. What with overcrowding and the shortness of funds, the big city schools have a very steep uphill climb when it comes to educating their students.

"But here, with so few students in each classroom, we'll have the time to not only learn the mandated material, we'll be able to tackle other projects, projects that interest you—projects that could never be possible in the school I left behind."

"So, what kind of 'projects' do you have in mind?" another boy asked, suspicion evident in his voice. "Does this mean we'll be working harder than those city kids have to?"

"I wouldn't say 'harder' so much as more

effectively."

"Which means?" the first boy asked. The expression on his face reflected an unwillingness to do anything not absolutely state mandated.

"I think we'll decide that after we've gotten to know one another better. For now, we'll stay with the material the state requires of all of its twelfth grade classes. Then, after I get a feel of what sort of things 'turn you on', we'll start thinking about what we'd like to do as a class."

"Oh! So you're only talking about us seniors," a pretty little blond girl sitting in the second row said. "I don't think it's fair that we're going to be the only grade that has to do extra work."

"Actually, that's not how it's going to go. I'll be offering extra credit work to all grade levels. I only mentioned the seniors because this particular class is made up of that grade level."

"Well, that's better," the girl said as she settled more comfortably into her chair. "I just didn't want to be the only ones having to knock ourselves out."

Hum, things were not exactly going as Eden had hoped. Perhaps she'd overestimated the students, expecting them to be infused with the same excitement she herself felt. That was okay. Before she was finished with them, they'd be begging to be included in her special projects.

The rest of the week went by rather quietly as Eden and her students got to know each other. Assignments were given and returned to her—some more spectacularly done than others. The original tensions melted away as the kids came to know Eden, realizing that although she was a stickler for work, she also had a raucous sense of humor and had no fear in sharing it with her students. By the second week, a few of the students began asking about the special projects she had mentioned that first day, thinking that perhaps this new teacher of theirs might actually have some good ideas after all.

"Okay," she said at the start of class after they'd been together for almost a month, "several of you have been asking about how they could earn extra credits in my classes. Does anyone have any ideas of what you'd like to do?"

Several hands flew up, actually more of them than she had expected.

"Todd, did you have something you'd like to suggest?"

"Yeah! How about writing a school newspaper? That would come under 'English', wouldn't it? I could write the sports column."

"Oh, right! Since we don't have enough guys to put together a football time, what did you have in mind—a coed team?" Johnny Wilson quipped.

"I wouldn't mind," Todd replied, a grin splitting his face.

"I bet you wouldn't," Leslie Jordan, the cute blond who had made the second row seat her own personal domain replied. "But you can just forget that. There's not a girl in this school dumb enough to let you teenage perverts tackle her, so you can just forget about writing about our school's non-existent sporting glory."

"A school paper isn't a bad idea," Eden came to Todd's defense. "Would anyone else be interested in writing a column?"

"Get Janie to write an advice column," Johnnie suggested. "She's always more than willing to tell everyone what they ought to do."

"Hey! Just because I have more common sense than you, doesn't mean you get to make fun of me," Janie Ingleson replied, her voice containing more than a bit of resentment.

"And we could always get the schools biggest gossips to write the "What's Happening at Gold Bluff High" column," another of the boys suggested in a wry tone.

"I don't like this newspaper idea," Janie said sullenly. "Whoever writes a column could get in a lot of trouble if people don't like what they write. And then there you'd be, seeing them every day in school, and them mad at you and all."

"Janie does have a point," Eden said. "Printing what needs to be said does not always make a journalist popular. But reporting the news is an important job, one that should always be taken seriously. It's not something that should be thought of as a joke. Now, does anyone else have a suggestion?"

"How about….? No …. That wouldn't be so good."

"Could we, like, put on a play?" Leslie asked.

"Oh, right! And you'll play the lead, right?" Todd grinned at the pretty blond.

"Yeah! Let's do Romeo and Juliet. I volunteer to be Romeo if Leslie plays Juliet," Johnnie said with a very definite leer in his voice.

"You know, a play isn't such a bad idea," Eden broke in. "But I think we should write our own play."

"Write a play!"

"You gotta' be kidding."

"We couldn't do something like that! What could we ever write about that would be interesting enough for people to want to come see us make fools of ourselves?"

"We see you do it all the time, make a fool of yourself, that is."

Eden was beginning to think she'd made a huge mistake by voicing her opinion until she realized the comments being thrown about the room were done in a spirit of fun rather than unkindness.

"Actually, I was thinking we might kill two birds with one stone with this project. I was thinking we could write a play about the history of our very own town. That way you could earn extra credits in both of my classes, both

English *and* history."

"Would we really put the play on for people to come and see?"

"I don't see why not. I bet the townspeople would get a real kick out of seeing their own town's history reenacted by you guys."

"Wow! That *would* be kind of cool, wouldn't it?" The oh-so-cool Todd said with a tone of awe in his voice. "I mean, we've all heard that this place was settled by some very heavy dudes. It might be a blast to find out all about them, then get to 'be' them in the play."

Before she knew what had happened, the entire classroom was caught up in the idea. She glanced at the clock on the wall—only ten minutes left before the bell would ring. She smiled as she saw the excitement take hold and decided that there would be no better way to spend those last few minutes than to let them run with the idea of writing their own play about the town they all lived in.

Chapter Six

Sam Gorton groaned inwardly each time he saw one of Eden's students walking by with notebook and pen at the ready. Even in his worst nightmares, he had never considered that she might actually give those kids the assignment of researching Gold Bluff's history. Yee gods, could she have come up with a worse idea? He seriously doubted it.

"Mr. Gorton, would you mind if I interviewed you for our play?"

Sam's silent groaning stepped up a notch as he looked into the guileless eyes of little Leslie Jordan. What the heck was he supposed to do now?

"Why, sure, honey. I'd love to fill you in on all I know about it. Have you read the brochure our Chamber of Commerce printed up? It's all there—at least all that I know about."

"But you must know a lot of stuff that's not in the brochure. After all, you've been here for just about forever, haven't you?"

"Well now, that's not exactly true. I spent a lot of time around these parts when I was a kid, but I can't say as I learned much about the real history of the area. You know, most of the really interesting stuff happened a long time ago—way before my family and I started coming here."

"So, can you suggest anyone I should talk to about it?"

She was a persistent little thing, he had to give her that. He wondered how elevated her grade would be if he made up some really shocking 'real life' events for her to take back to Eden.

There had been a time in his life when he would have done just that, just for the heck of it. But that was a long time ago. Now he was the guy who told nothing but the truth—well, almost nothing.

"I suppose I should be asking old Tom these questions," she said as she closed her notebook and put away her pen. "He's the only one—him and Uncle Billy, of course—who know all that much about what went on during the gold rush days."

"No! Don't…. that is, well, you know how old men can be. Their memories sometimes get confused. They can get fact and fiction all mixed up, until they can't tell one from the other."

"Oh, that might be true of some old people, but I don't think Tom and Billy are like that. Why, my dad says those two old men are as sharp as they come. He says their stories about the old days are better than most movies."

Sam felt his stomach tighten. Better than movies? You bet they were! And just about as apt to be true. He watched the young student walk away from him, wishing with all his heart he could call her back and set her straight. But there was nothing he could do but stand back and watch his world disintegrate before his eyes.

Suddenly he had an idea—a really, *really,* great idea. One he couldn't believe he hadn't thought of earlier. He'd just have to use all his charm on the comely new school marm and head her and her students off before they'd learned enough to ruin him and all of his cohorts. He'd romance all thoughts of history right out of her mind.

No, maybe romance wasn't the right word. Charm, yeah, that was more like it. He'd only try to romance Eden if he was interested in her, well, *romantically.* And he wasn't. Not really... As far as Eden McKenna was concerned, his only interest in her was business.

Suddenly he knew the lie for what it was. Damn right, he was interested in Eden…had been from the first moment he'd laid eyes on her. The only question now was, what was he going to do about it?

*****

"I'd really love to have dinner with you, Sam but are you certain it would be appropriate? I mean, would this be a business meeting or would it be of a more social nature?"

"Social, strictly social."

"If that's the case, then I'm afraid I'll have to turn you down—with regrets, of course. I make it a rule to never fraternize with my superiors."

"But my dear Ms. McKenna…Eden…that would most definitely not be the case, since I have resigned my position on the School Board this very day. The dinner invitation comes solely from Sam Gorton, real estate dealer, mayor of Gold Bluff and *former* head of the School Board."

"But as mayor, wouldn't that also qualify as fraternization?"

"Not at all, not at all. As mayor I have absolutely nothing to do with how our schools are run. Although I am still on the board, my new position has nothing to do with personnel. From today on I'll be working entirely with building and maintenance issues."

"Well, if that's the case, Mr. Gorton, then I suppose I am free to accept your invitation."

Her smile was the prettiest thing he had seen in a very long time. How did she manage to look so innocent and yet so damned sexy at the same time, he wondered? Was it something she practiced or did it come naturally?

*****

"Ms. McKenna, we're all having trouble getting interviews with people old enough around here to remember much about Gold Bluff's 'good old days.' Every time I find someone who looks old enough to know something, it turns out they've only been here a year or two themselves, just like my own family. Do you have any ideas of where we should go from here?"

"Have you tried the local library? There should be plenty of information there. And then there's always the weekly newspaper, the Gold Bluff Clarion. They should have archives going back to the paper's first issue."

"Todd and I tried the library," Leslie spoke up, "but they weren't any help at all. They had information on the history of Siskiyou County, but nothing much about the Gold Bluff area. Gosh, after checking through all those old books and finding not one single thing about our town, you'd think we never actually existed before the year 2000. They must have been pretty bad about keeping records back in those days."

Eden had combined her senior English and history classes into one two hour period so the students could work on their project better. They all had agreed that if they were going to do the play, they needed to get as organized as possible, which included researching, writing, staging, and creating costumes.

It took no time at all for the students' enthusiasm for the play to engulf the entire town. It seemed that everyone in town wanted to be a part of it. When Uncle Billy heard about the project, he quickly volunteered to help the woodshop teacher build the stage and everything else that would be needed for the presentation. It had been his idea to forgo using the school's gym for the production, with folding chairs lined up on the basketball court and a makeshift stage at the far end.

"What kind of stage would that be?" he'd asked scornfully after he'd listened to the shop teacher describe what he intended to put together. "If you're going to do something as ambitious as the re-creation of our town's history, you need to have a proper stage to present it on."

"Yeah, what you need is an amphitheater," Tom had suggested.

As was so often the case, the pair of old codgers had once again placed themselves right in the middle of the town's most popular coffee shop, where just about everything important that happened in Gold Bluff was discussed. Forget about city council or chamber of commerce meetings. If something was important it got taken care of at the High Trails Café.

"Here, Mary, give me a refill," Tom lifted his coffee mug to the passing waitress, "while I get a handle on this here historical saga. After all, this *is* all about my people, right? As such, I do believe I should have a say in how and where it's presented."

"Now, Tom," the shop teacher tried to interrupt, "don't be getting this thing way out of proportion. It's just a high school assignment, not some Hollywood production."

"Spoken by a man who probably doesn't know where his own ancestors are buried," Tom replied gruffly. "If those kids are going to do a play about the Wenton family, then by God, I got a right to say where it's going to be put on. And I say we need to give those kids a stage worthy of their efforts."

"And I suppose you know just where you want this stage?" Billy asked dryly.

"I do. In fact, it's my intention to donate the perfect place for it. If Ms. Eden agrees, I intend to give the town my ten acres at the very foot of Gold Bluff—right where the very first gold nuggets were found."

"Says you," Sam said as he strolled up to the table where Tom and Billy were holding court.

"And you, if I recall," Tom gave him a steely expression which suggested he was not at all likely to let himself be backed down.

Sam winced.

"I don't remember you denying any of what went into that brochure the partners handed out when we were putting this town on the map."

"Oh, let it go, Tom. Sam didn't mean anything, did you, Sam?" Billy tried to shush the two up. Several of the other tables were filled with people none of the old timers recognized, and he wasn't at all pleased by the curious expressions that were being directed their way. "Sam, Tom just wants to give the kids a little help, that's all."

"Yeah, right," Sam replied, his tone indicating his disbelief.

"But you got to admit, that spot Tom's offering would make a damned nice little amphitheater."

"Building a stage and benches would be a great project for my class," the shop teacher added, enthusiasm evident in his voice. "Heck, this thing could be a real asset to our community."

"Mary, forget the coffee and bring me a beer," Sam called to the waitress. "No, better make that two beers. From the way things are going, one beer is definitely not going to be enough.

*****

Sam placed his hand at the small of Eden's back, directing her down the center aisle of the McCloud Dinner Train's second dining car, leading her to the table at the rear of the car. Strains of classic jazz played by a small combo in the next car could be heard each time the doors of the two cars happened to be opened simultaneously. Sam had heard stories about the train's elegance and was pleased to see he hadn't been misled. If a man wanted to impress a woman, there wasn't any other place in the entire county that could equal this.

'Wow, if you're trying to impress me, you've done it." Eden said as she sat down in the chair he held for her. "This is absolutely fabulous!"

"I hope you like train rides. I'm told this one can get a bit bumpy."

"Well, why wouldn't it? Considering that everything about it is authentic—including the track!"

"Suitable for a history buff like yourself?" he asked as he poured champagne into the crystal flute she held out to him.

"More than suitable," she replied before sipping the wine. "Umm, this champagne is wonderful." She smiled at him over the rim of her glass. Although Eden was far from an expert on the subject, she recognized that the champagne was of a remarkably good vintage.

"And you, Sam, are you interested in history too? Or is all of this," she indicated the contents of the train car with her hand that held the champagne glass, "just meant to impress me?"

"Since history was never one of my better subjects, I suppose I'll have to admit to the latter."

"Well, I must say, you've done a good job of it. So far, that is." Her easy laughter brought a smile to his lips.

"Just wait 'till they bring the food. I hear they have the best steaks in the state."

Just then the train pulled out of the picturesque town's station, heading into the thickly forested mountain canyon. The meal was served with elaborate care, each morsel completely living up to its reputation.

The sun set as they finished their meal. With a smile, Sam suggested they retreat to the lounge car. At the far end of the car, the musical combo was now playing dance music. Without saying a word, Sam opened his arms, inviting Eden to join him in a slow, romantic dance. The music, though not authentic to the train's original era, was vintage '40s, the sort of music Fred Astaire and Ginger Rogers had favored in so many of their movies.

As far as Eden was concerned, the night could not have been more magical. The dinner had been superb, the train a delight, and the feel of Sam's arms around her the most sensual experience she'd had in a very long time.

She couldn't have said if she had stepped closer into his embrace because of his urging or her own, but it seemed the most natural thing in the world to do. She took a deep breath, taking in the very essence of him. Umm, divine!

Closing her eyes, she let him lead her where he would, around and around, until, with a sharp lurch of the train she found herself pinned very firmly against his chest.

"I paid the engineer to do that," his soft voice whispered in her ear.

"Oh? And just when I was thinking of doing the very same thing." Not bothering to hide her smile, she tilted her head back so she could gaze into his eyes.

The angle she held her head brought her lips into a very tempting position—too tempting for Sam to refuse. Lowering his head, he captured her lips in a very gentle kiss.

Being very aware of where they were, he did not allow the kiss to deepen to the depth he would have liked, pulling back while still craving more. He leaned back from her a moment, gathering his breath as he looked away. He pulled her closer for the briefest of moments, then allowed space to come between them once again.

"Maybe we should go out on the observation deck for a while", he suggested. "I only paid the engineer to do that once—figured I might make a fool of myself if it happened again."

She hesitated and then slipped out of his arms and allowed him to guide her out of the back of the car where they joined several other couples who were sitting on benches on a flat car, most of them gazing raptly at the star strewn heavens.

"You know," he said, his voice still not quite as firm as usual, "history can be overrated at times."

"How do you mean? From my experience, we can all benefit from learning more of what went on before us."

"Oh, right! After all, if we don't study history we're destined to make the same mistakes over and over again. I get all that. What I was talking about was, well, take a place like Gold Bluff. We know there were people who came before us—strong, capable people."

"Oh my, yes. From what I've read in Tom's mother's journal, the Wenton's were of extremely strong stock."

"But how important is it that we learn all about them? I mean, can't we just take old Tom at his word about what happened all those years ago?"

"Well, yes, we could, of course. But then we'd miss out on the excitement of discovery. I can't tell you how excited I was when I first opened Etta Wenton's journal. You can't imagine how thrilled I was to be able to read her very own words—her thoughts!"

"But..."

'When I read those pages, I'm not living in the twenty-first century any more. I'm living her life, dreaming her dreams, sharing her memories. Oh, Sam, I wish I could share the wonder of it with you."

"Well..."

"And that's what I want my students to discover. I want them to feel what I feel. I want them to become a part of the history. This is their town, Sam. I want them to own it right down to their toes!"

"Their toes, yeah, right... their toes."

So much for his romancing Eden away from her commitment to this darned Gold Bluff saga she had going. If anything, the date, which he had hoped to use as a way to distract her from her cause, had done just the opposite. What had he been thinking? Did he really believe she was such an airhead that a little champagne and romantic dancing would distract a woman like Eden? If there was an airhead on the train, he knew who it was—and it wasn't Eden McKenna.

*****

"You know, Ms. McKenna, if Gold Bluff was such a big deal back in the gold rush days, wouldn't you think there'd be some mention of it in the county records? I've spent over eight hours searching through those dusty old files and I haven't found word one about it. Heck, I haven't even found the name 'Gold Bluff' listed any earlier than the early nineteen hundreds. I'm beginning to wonder if there ever really was a gold strike out here." George, one of Eden's senior students looked about as frustrated as a toddler trying to get a cookie off the counter that he couldn't quite reach.

"Are you sure the clerk gave you the right files?" Eden hadn't expected the search for local information to be a total breeze, but she sure as heck hadn't expected it to be this difficult. For just a moment she wondered if she had bitten off more than her students could chew.

Still concerned she might have set her students an impossible task, she mentioned her worries later that afternoon to Tom Wenton. "It seems so strange that none of the kids are coming up with anything concrete about the beginning of Gold Bluff. I was wondering if maybe you could come to my class tomorrow and give them a little help. It would be great if they could hear your stories about the Wenton's."

"Why, I'd love to, honey," Tom's eyes glowed with anticipation. "There's nothing I like more than talking about my family. That is unless it's getting old Billy's goat over something. What time would you like me to come?"

*****

"No! I absolutely forbid it. Under no circumstances are you to go into that classroom and fill those kids' heads with a bunch of nonsense."

"Now, Sam, you can't forbid me anything. Or have you forgotten that you aren't the School Superintendent anymore? You know, I've been wondering just why it was you gave up that job anyway. Couldn't have something to do with our new little school marm, could it?"

Sam knew Tom was just baiting him but the ribbing still got to him. So what if he had given up the School Board job so he'd have a clear path to Eden's doorstep.

What business was it of anyone's but his?

Actually what was really bugging him was that even though he was no longer Eden's boss, he hadn't made much headway in the romance department with her. Except for that one very chaste kiss on the dinner train, he hadn't had the nerve to even touch her.

"Okay, you're right, I can't order you to stay out of her classroom, but I can ask you not to do it—as a favor to me, if not for her. It just isn't right for you to go in there and fill her students' heads with a bunch of garbage."

Tom gave Sam one of his most baleful looks; the one that almost never failed to put his opponent on the ropes. "You really hurt me when you say things like that, Sam. Why, I'm just about the most truthful man in this here town. Your words really pain me."

Sam just sighed. He should have known he wouldn't get anywhere appealing to Tom's better instincts. When it came to being the center of attention, Tom Wenton knew no shame.

*****

Eden looked over her classroom, letting her eyes settle on the visitor who stood at the very back of the room. Why, she wondered, would Sam Gorton ask to be there when Tom gave his talk? She had readily agreed, of course; what reason could she have to refuse him? But still, it seemed odd to her he would have any interest in what Tom had to say. Surely, he must know the story of the Wenton family almost as well as Tom did by now. Hadn't he said they'd known one another since Sam had been a young boy?

In the moment she allowed her gaze to lock with Sam's she felt a charge of electricity pass between them that was so strong she feared her students might have noticed. As her gaze locked with his, she felt herself grinning at him. When he returned her smile, she thought she might melt into a helpless puddle right there in front of

God and the world. His smile broadened, as if he knew exactly how she felt.

This was not good. This was most definitely not good. She was supposed to be up here teaching her students, not making an utter fool of herself in front of them.

A giggle from one of the girls in the front row brought her back to her classroom with a start. Her overly responsive complexion glowed at the realization that she could hide very few secrets from these bright kids. Glancing back at Sam she couldn't help but smile when he gave her a what-can-I-say shrug and smile. Not a thing, Mr. Gorton, not a thing, her replying half smile and lifted eyebrow replied.

*****

To his credit, he felt a stab of remorse that he had thrown her a curve like that. But were he to be strictly honest about it, he would have to admit it was a very tiny one. The good guy side of him knew he had no right coming here if it meant that his presence would in any way disrupt Eden's classroom. But his other side, the side that was driven by a very healthy male ego, couldn't have been more pleased by Eden's reaction.

Of course, romancing the teacher had not been the reason for his visit. What brought him here was strictly business. Even though all of the others thought he was overreacting to Tom's irresponsible tricks, he knew deep down in his gut that somebody had to keep an eye on the old coot. And, apparently, since no one else had volunteered for the job, that somebody was him.

*****

"As you all know, we have a very special guest today," Eden said, turning her attention back to the class. "Although I doubt that any of you don't already know him, I'd like to introduce Mr. Tom Wenton. Tom is, as I understand it, the only direct descendent left of the original founding family of Gold Bluff. Tom…?" She stepped to the side of the room, allowing the old man to take center front.

Sam stood stock still, not daring to breath. What outrageous lies was the old coot going to spread, he worried. And what, if anything, could he do to stop him?

"Well, hi there everyone," Tom said as he glanced from one young face to another. "Seems as if I've seen every one of you around town at some time or other. So I feel right at home standing up here talking to you.

"I've been hearing that you all have decided to do a little research about this town—and about my family—for a play you'll be putting on. And, that you've been having trouble getting all your facts straight. Lucky for you, I'm the one and only person around here who knows it all. My old granny, she told me the story from the time I was old enough to sit on her lap.

"Now, let's see, where should I start? Umm, I guess right at the beginning would be best. All right, here we go.

"The first Wenton that came this way was my very own Grandpappy, Jedidiah Wenton. He came here by a rickety old wagon over the Oregon Trail in the year of 1852. He brought along his new wife—she was just a girl of sixteen at the time—and a wagon full of farm tools.

"From what she told me, my Grandpappy was so strong minded about getting a good start with the farm, that he hadn't allowed her enough space to bring much of anything for herself or for their first home—just a couple of dresses, two quilts her mother'd made for her hope chest and enough cooking gear to make up a pot of beans and a mess of biscuits.

"You girls can sympathize with her. I can't say as I could imagine you pretty young things settling for only having two or three dresses in your closets. But then, my poor granny didn't even have a closet for her things, so I guess you can't compare."

"Why did they choose this place?" one of the boys asked.

"Well, as I recall, Grandpappy said it wasn't so much that they chose it as that it chose them. They was heading up north from Sacramento. The going was tough, but the weather hadn't been too bad, so they figured they were going to make it to Oregon in fairly good time. Then, in the last week of October, it started snowing.

"He wasn't all that worried at first. After all, how much snow could there be that early in the winter? But he didn't know how rough it can get up here in the Cascades. All he'd really heard in regards to the California mountains were the Sierra Nevadas. And yes, he had heard of the Donner party.

"Anyways, it snowed so much that pretty soon they lost track of the trail, wandering off to the east of where they should'a been. After a while he realized they were lost, but by then they'd come down out of the worst of the storm into the prettiest little valley he'd ever seen. After talking it over with my granny, the two of them decided that Oregon couldn't possibly be better than where they were, so they unloaded their wagon, set up camp, and made themselves to home.

"And that's how my family first came to Gold Bluff."

"But you didn't say anything about them finding the bluffs. I've been to their farm, and it's miles away from the bluffs." Another of the boys commented.

"That it was. Actually, they never saw the bluffs until a year or so later. And it wasn't the bluffs that was of interest to them then, only that their valley would be a good place to set up their farm, or ranch, as it ended up being."

"Tell us about how the gold was found," one of the girls urged.

"Well, that's another story … a really sad story, as a matter of fact.

"My granddaddy and granny were doing fairly well, raising food for the table and nice fat cattle and a whole passel of young'uns. Let's see, they had nine children, one set of triplets amongst them."

"Right! And she had those triplets all by herself, right? I heard that the only one there to help her with their birth was her five-year-old son and an Indian brave," another of the girls called out.

Sam closed his eyes and shook his head. Why hadn't old Tom gone into fiction writing, he wondered? What with all the tall tales he told, he could have been another Mark Twain.

"Right you are! But that's another story. I was going to tell you about the gold."

"Yeah, go on. We'd rather hear about the gold, wouldn't we, guys?"

"Okay, yeah, right. Well, actually the two sort of have something to do with each other. You see, when granny had those three babies, as you said, young lady, Grandpappy was off selling some cattle. He didn't know Granny was carrying triplets, and that multiple births often are born earlier than expected. Anyway, he'd left her there at the ranch, thinking she had a couple more months to go before he'd have to worry about the baby.

"He'd been gone a couple of days when Granny knew the baby was on its way—well, actually the babies. She'd already had a couple of kids, one of 'um being the five-year-old boy you mentioned. The other one, another boy, who happened to be my very own daddy, was little more than two-years-old and no help at all. In fact he was worse than no help, from the stories I've heard about him.

"She didn't know what to do. All she could think was to send her oldest boy down the trail that led to the lake at the end of the valley, hoping he'd find one of the Indians who lived in the hills out beyond there. And that's what happened. When my uncle got to the lake there was this Indian skinning a deer he'd just killed. He told the Indian what his mother said—that she needed help with a baby. Only the Indian, he didn't understand English all that well. So, instead of going back to his village to get one of the women, he went to the ranch himself.

"Now, as far as I know, Indian men know even less about birthing babies than my Granny did. But, he must 'a been fairly bright, because he got her to lay down, calmed her down as best he could without the two of them knowing the other's language, and then he left her there."

"He left her all alone?"

"That's what Granny thought he was doing, but what he did was to go back to his village and bring her the help she needed. He brought two old Indian women with him. My Granny called them her two brown angels. They took over, helping her all the way until those babies were born screaming their lungs out like little piglets, 'stead of the underweight critters they were."

"But what does that have to do with the gold?"

"I'm getting there," Tom responded with a twinkle in his eye.

"My old Grandpappy was forever in those Indians' debt, and he never forgot it. From that day forward, he treated the whole village like they were family, and they responded in kind. Then, about five, no make that six years later, six years and four more babies, something terrible happened that changed everything forever.

"There'd been some bad things happening in the vicinity. A bunch of ruffians, really more outlaws than anything else, decided that the Indians didn't belong there anymore. They'd been plaguing the dickens out of several Indian villages, driving them off their land, killing them for any excuse they could think of. In fact, there'd been a couple of villages completely wiped out in recent months.

"Well, Grandpappy, he couldn't abide that sort of thing. He and Granny were sick every time they heard about something happening to the natives, but their one consolation was that their own Indian friends had not been targeted. Then it happened, those thugs took it into their heads to take on the native village just south of the Wenton ranch.

"Someone came out to the ranch and told Grandpappy there'd been talk that their village had been targeted, and that before long he'd be able to lay claim to the land left behind by the dead Indians. Apparently, the man who carried the tale was fool enough to think Grandpappy would be grateful. In fact, as I recall, there was talk that Grandpappy should give them money for doing the deed for him.

"He told the man in words strong enough that Granny put her hands over her youngest boy's ears what he thought of anyone who would do such a dastardly deed. Although he hoped his words would be enough to save his friends, he feared they would not, so he headed out to the village to warn his friends of the impending attack, taking with him a couple of rifles he felt he could spare.

"Fortunately, they already had some weapons, so, what with his warning, and the extra rifles, they were ready when the attack came. They fought the raiders off, killing their leader, which was a lucky thing because without him the others just sort of lost their taste for Indian blood.

"The sad thing was, though, that even though they didn't feel like killing any more Indians, they did feel like killing the man they figured was responsible for their failure—my Grandpappy. After they'd gotten themselves suitably drunk later that night, the bunch of them skulked back to the Wenton ranch. They hid out there, waiting 'til first dawn when they figured Grandpappy would come out to feed the animals. He no sooner stepped out the door than they let loose with a barrage of bullets that would' a killed a dozen men, had they been standing there."

"They killed him?" one of the girls asked, tears

glistening in her eyes.

"That they did."

"But what happened to your Granny and all those children?"

"That's where the gold part of the story comes in. The head Indian over at that village, he felt so darned bad about what had happened to Grandpappy after how he'd helped them out, he decided he had to help Granny.

"Now, he knew the great store white man put on gold, which the Indians thought was just plain stupid, since you couldn't eat or drink the stuff. Anyways, his people had known about a place not far from the Wenton ranch that was loaded with it. He and his village decided that what they should do was to tell Granny about the gold so that she could use it to help with the kids."

"Did she actually mine the gold herself?"

"Her and the kids. She was a smart cookie, my Granny. She put in her claim, all right and proper. She and the oldest boys got to work and dug out enough gold to pay for the help she needed on the ranch so's she and her family never had to worry about losing their home."

"But why worry about a ranch when you have a gold mine?"

"That's what tells you how smart my Granny was. She figured that the gold vein would most likely run out eventually, but the ranch could support her family forever. As long as she had all those mouths to feed, she was not about to let that ranch go. No, she kept the ranch *and* she kept the mine."

"I've been all over these mountains and seen all those old buildings out at the ranch, but I've never seen any gold mine around here," one of the boys observed.

"And you most likely never will," Tom said with a wicked smile.

"But, why? Man, I'd sure like to get a look at it."

"And so would a great many others. But, as I said

before, my old Granny, she was as smart as they come. She and her boys, they were the only people other than the Indians who ever knew exactly where that mine was located. There've been many a prospector that tried to locate it and failed."

"But, when she staked the claim, she registered it, right? If she had, couldn't someone look it up?"

"Sure they could. But, if, and this is a big if, there was anything in the records, that still wouldn't necessarily make it possible to find it. You've got to remember, that was pretty wild country out there—still is. Just because you know the general area of where it's located, you still couldn't find it if the entrance to the mine was hidden well enough."

"So, there really is a hidden gold mine somewhere around Gold Bluff?"

"Would I lie?" Tom asked, his face the image of innocence.

Still standing at the back of the classroom, Sam listened to Tom's every word. Too worried about the lies the old man might feed the kids, he couldn't have left had he wanted to. By the time Tom had finished his tale, all Sam could do was close his eyes and groan. To his credit, he managed to keep the groan silent.

Chapter Seven

Eden couldn't believe the far reaching effects the seniors' project would have on the city of Gold Bluff. Everywhere you looked you saw young people involved in the project in one way or another. And it went far beyond her students.

After Tom's speech to her class, the shop teacher happily told her he had been swamped with volunteers to help build the new outdoor amphitheater. When she considered that the land Tom had donated for the theater abutted the famous gold bluffs themselves, she was not exactly surprised to learn about the sudden interest. After all, Tom had all but said outright that the missing gold mine had been located somewhere in that very same region. What enterprising young man worth his salt would not be excited about being allowed—even encouraged—to dig in that yellow hued earth. Heck, she wouldn't mind doing a little digging herself. What fun it would be to find a gold nugget!

And, in less than one week after the construction project had begun, that was exactly what happened. Not to Eden, but to one of the students. He had been working off to one side of the construction area, clearing away soil where the backstage dressing area would ultimately be, when he noticed several small, yellow pebbles. Only they weren't pebbles—they were honest-to-goodness gold nuggets.

He let out a whoop that put a stop to the work and drew a large audience to his side. When he showed them what he had found, more shovels suddenly appeared and the entire work crew set to digging a huge hole at the site, being very careful to examine each shovel-full of soil.

All in all, eleven more nuggets were found before the sun sat that evening, forcing the work to be put off until the following day. The next day all of the teachers at Gold

Bluff High noted a very distinct disinterest in studies. The final bell had not stopped ringing when the front doors burst open and at least fifty students, both male and female, pushed their way out and headed to the "diggin's".

"You know what he's done, don't you?" Sam glowered at his partners as they all sat around the table in the High Trails Café's back room. "He salted that so called mine of his, that's what he's done."

"Now, Sammy old boy, you don't know that for a fact," Joe Stanton pointed out.

"Oh, don't I? You weren't in that classroom while he filled those kids' heads full of this gold rush crap. You didn't see him bait them the way I did."

"Maybe it was all true, Sam. Maybe there really was a gold mine out there at the bluffs," Mason tried to reason.

"Yeah, and the Easter bunny lays golden eggs."

"From where I sit," Joe interrupted, "I don't see that it matters much if old Tom was making up another one of his whoppers or not. We all knew from the beginning the old guy liked to stretch the truth a bit. I doubt that anyone in town actually believes everything he says"

"So what do we do about this gold mine business?" Sam asked the other land development partners. "You must all agree we can't just let things go on like this."

"That's exactly what we have to do. If we try to stop it, things will definitely get very complicated around here. But if we just let the yarn run itself out, why in a couple of weeks or so everyone will have completely forgotten about it. After all, how many nuggets could the old boy have tossed out there?"

Actually, no one ever knew if Tom had actually salted the area or not. But if he had, he must have done a fairly good job of it because, before the kids got tired of digging, forty-three nuggets of various sizes were found. Some thought there were more, but after a full week of digging had produced no more gold, the project returned to what it had originally been—the building of the Gold Bluff Amphitheater.

    When the gold rush was finally over, Sam had to admit that nothing really serious had come out of it, other than a larger dressing room area than the original plans had called for. Actually, the entire stage area, including the backstage, was far larger than had originally been planned. But after looking over the gaping hole left behind by the "miners" it was decided to make use of their labor by enlarging the original blueprints.

*****

    It was a beautiful moonlit night. Though the early November night was cool, Eden barely felt the evening's chill. She'd left her house dressed for a long walk, wearing sturdy boots and jacket as well as warm woolen slacks. It was well past the dinner hour, over an hour since the sun had set. The site would, hopefully, be deserted.

    Something pulled her to the amphitheater, the place where all the frantic activity had been going on for the last three weeks. Even though it was far from finished there was a certain order to it. The stage area was starting to take form, as was the area where the audience would one day sit. A deep indentation into the lovely golden hued bluffs had been dug, making a shell shape over the area where the future actors would perform. Facing the bluffs, the audience seating was beginning to take shape. The hill that rose beyond the bluffs had been perfect for the step-like seating. It took very little imagination for her to visualize the actors down on the stage, their voices rising to the audience that sat just beyond the footlights. It would not be a huge venue, but the very intimacy of it would make each presentation special.

    Caught up in her reverie, she walked slowly down the steps that had been cut into the hillside, walking toward the stage. It still amazed her that all of this was happening.

Never in her wildest dreams would she have thought any of this would have been possible that first day she'd come to Gold Bluff. How could she have guessed during her interview with Sam that she would one day be standing here, gazing at the beginnings of a building that would be a permanent part of this wonderful community? It almost frightened her to realize her ideas had led to this.

Suddenly she realized she was not alone. There, deep back in the farthest reaches of the indentation—the kids called it the cave—she saw a man. He was kneeling down, as if he were searching for something. In his crouching position, she could not see who he was.

She began to turn away, hoping he would not see her. Nobody knew she had come out here. Maybe it hadn't been such a good idea for her to walk all this way by herself. She'd felt safe in Gold Bluff, so much more so than she ever had while living in the city. Had that sense of safety allowed her to let her defenses down when she should have been more cautious? She felt her heart speed up, her breathing become shallow.

Then the man stood and her heart began to race like crazy. If it was danger she feared, then she really did have something to be worried about because the man who stood there in the shadows was most definitely a very dangerous man. He was a man who could steal a woman's heart, if she were not careful. A man whose smile alone could make a woman forget every form of self-defense she'd ever learned. The man was no other than Sam Gorton.

In the weeks that had passed since their dinner date on the train she had seen Sam numerous times around town. They always spoke…hello…how've you been...or, how are those kids treating you? Always pleasant, yet also impersonal. She was always pleased to see him, yet was also pleased to see him pass on by.

It was as if they were playing a sort of game with each other. It reminded her of when she used to play with magnets when she had been a child. It had always fascinated her how, if she held the magnets one way they were forcibly drawn together, but if she turned the other way the same energy forced them apart. To add to the magic of the magnets, she noted that if they were placed so that their magnetic poles were facing in the same direction, the little pieces of metal were neither drawn together nor repelled.

Whenever she was near Sam, it was as if they were those magnets, their poles facing in the same direction. The constant shifting of energy confused Eden, made her feel out of control. And, since she didn't like being out of control she had done the only thing she could think of, which was to avoid contact with him as much as possible.

Avoiding close contact had been easy enough. All she had to do was to make sure they were never alone. But now, here in the dark, just the two of them…

Maybe if she walked very quietly he wouldn't see her, she thought as she started to back step away from him. She'd been avoiding being alone with him ever since their date on the dinner train.

It wasn't that she hadn't enjoyed herself that night, because she had—very much. That was exactly why she'd been working so hard to stay away from him. The man was simply too handsome—too smooth—and very definitely too sexy. He was way out of her league. And he scared her half to death because she knew that if she allowed herself she could fall very hard for him. And that was something she simply would not do.

She'd always been the studious type, too busy with her studies to pursue much of a social life. Sure, she'd been asked out on dates, plenty of them. And she'd gone on a few, mostly with men who shared her interests in books and history. But she'd always avoided the "big man on campus" types, knowing instinctively that to date one of them would be to court disaster.

What would they talk about, football? Who was dating whom? Where the next wild party would be held? What a bunch of tripe! She had better ways of using her time than subjecting herself to such nonsense.

She was not the type of girl who enjoyed that type of dating. And she had absolutely no doubt she would bore those guys half to death too. Better to stay at home with her books than to waste either her time or theirs.

If she'd ever doubted that decision, she had only to look at her parent's marriage to prove her point of not mixing what she called the "social" types with the "book" types. In her parent's case, it was her mother who was the one who needed the social life—a life filled with parties and exciting friends.

Luckily, her mom's job as head buyer for a chain of very exclusive dress shops gave her life the fulfillment she craved. To her daughter, Evelyn McKenna's life of constant traveling coupled with her full schedule of fashion shows and their accompanying parties, left little time for her family. When her mother had chosen to attend a business dinner rather than Eden's seventh birthday party, the little girl realized where she and her daddy fit into Evelyn's glamorous life… on the outside, looking in.

Fortunately for Eden, but unfortunately for the marriage, her father had never shared his wife's social cravings. While Evelyn took off with her friends for weeks of fashion shows and parties in Paris and London, her husband had been content to spend his time with his daughter, visiting museums or roaming through ghost towns. Patrick McKenna was Eden's mirror image intellectually, whereas her mother and she might have been total strangers.

Eden had always thought of their marriage as being sadly unfulfilled. She had made up her mind at a very early age that she'd rather not be married at all if it meant being married to someone whose interests varied so much from her own.

And no one, could be more different from her than Sam Gorton. So why let anything, even the tiniest thing, get started between them? It would be pointless—a disaster—a huge mistake.

But, oh, that kiss. Up until their lips touched, she had been absolutely certain being in his presence was perfectly safe for her. After all, he was very definitely not her type, right? He was the very essence of the sort of man she had spent her entire adult life trying to avoid. He was too handsome. He was far too charming. He was simply not for her.

She could not think of one thing they had in common, other than a shared love of the city of Gold Bluff and a sexual attraction to one another. She was basically an introverted intellectual, whereas Sam was the most extroverted person she had ever met. He'd had never shown a shred of interest in what mattered so dearly to her, the love of history. When it came to her, the main interest he'd shown was purely of the sexual nature.

No, they did not belong together. At least for the long haul, and Eden McKenna was not interested in romance that did not include at least the possibility of everlasting love. Considering all that, she was absolutely certain that any relationship she had with Sam Gorton would consist of nothing more than friendship.

But apparently he did not feel the same way about her. Why? What could he possibly see in her that he couldn't find in dozens of more willing women? *She* was the odd ball, not him. *She* was the one who would rather spend an evening with a good book than go out dancing and partying. Why, simply by looking at Sam you could tell he was more the partying type than the reading type. What in the world could he possibly see in her?

She took another step away from him, hoping to blend into the night before he saw her. But then, as if he somehow sensed her presence, he turned toward her. How could he possibly know she was there, she wondered? She'd been careful to not make a sound

"Is that you Eden?" His voice was quite strong—far too strong for her to pretend she had not heard him.

"Why, yes! Whatever are you doing there?" she answered back, deciding to put him on the defensive immediately.

"Just a little gold mining," he said with a sheepish grin that she could make out better as he came closer.

"In the dark? You must like working under a handicap."

"Well, yes, as a matter of fact I do," he replied. "Anyone worth his salt can find gold when the sun's out, don't you think?"

"Daylight would seem to give a person an advantage," she laughed. "But seriously, what were you finding so fascinating there in the dark?"

"Actually, I was telling you the truth. I *was* looking for nuggets. Although I must admit, I didn't expect to find any."

"But you were compelled to look anyway," she urged him on, a glimmer of humor shining in her eyes.

"Okay, okay, so I was being an idiot. Actually, like you, I was enjoying taking a walk in this beautiful moonlight and I just sort of found myself walking out this way. When I got close, I guess I got caught up in all the excitement that's been going on out here. I couldn't stop myself from pushing a little gravel around, hoping against hope that I'd see a spark of light shining back at me—that maybe the moonlight would reveal the one nugget that hadn't yet been found."

"You look like you'd just as soon I hadn't caught you at it. Why, if I didn't know better, Sam, I'd think you'd been caught with your hand in the cookie jar."

"Well, I do feel a little foolish letting myself be

caught looking for something I figure has been gone a very long time. That is, if this really *was* where the Wenton's gold mine was located."

"What makes you think this isn't the correct location? It would seem the recent finds would indicate this is the spot."

"So it would seem."

"You're doubtful."

"Is what I think all that important to you, Eden?"

"I think it's important to get all the historical facts possible, and that those facts be thoroughly authenticated. There's nothing I hate more than sloppy historical research."

"Ah, yes, history. Sometimes I wonder if you ever think of anything besides your beloved history," he sighed as he looked longingly into her eyes.

"I do! Why, I... I think of English, of course.... and my students... and...and..."

"But do you think of this?" he asked softly as he lowered his head toward her, slowly but deliberately closing the gap between their lips.

She knew she should step away from him. He wasn't the type of man who would push his advantage over a woman if she were to ask him to stop. All she had to do to keep him from kissing her would be to turn her head, to step back, to tell him to stop.

But the night was so beautiful, the moon shedding a mystical glow all around them. A slight breeze ruffled her hair, bringing with it the scent of pine trees and the first hint of rain. In the end, she simply stood there, waiting for the touch of his lips on hers. And when it came she knew she had made the mistake of a lifetime.

For some reason she had expected this kiss to be like the one he'd given her on the dinner train—sweet and undemanding. The sort of kiss that was given in public. What she had not expected was fireworks and a symphony of delightful sensations. What she had not expected was the answer to dreams she had not dared to dream. What she had definitely not expected was the sudden realization that if she lived to be a hundred, no other man in the world would kiss her as well as Sam Gorton was doing at that very moment.

"That may have been a mistake," was all she could say when he pulled away from her.

"Maybe, but I seriously doubt it."

"But…"

"No 'buts', Ms. McKenna. I've wanted to kiss that sweet mouth of yours from the first moment I saw you. And don't think that kiss on the train was what I'd been dreaming about. No, my dear Eden, this was the kiss I've been waiting for. And now that I've done it, I fully intend to do it again."

And she let him. For pity's sake, what was she thinking? She should stop him. But of course she didn't. Not that time, nor the next.

Chapter Eight

The field trip was, surprisingly, Sam's idea. When Eden mentioned she was trying to think of ways to help her students with their senior project, it was he who came up with the idea of a weekend trip out at the old Wenton ranch. Although it was November, the weather was still fairly mild, at least mild enough for a bunch of healthy young people to brave a couple of nights camping out.

"For some reason I got the idea you were against this project," Eden looked at him with a speculative gleam in her eye. "From the very beginning, it appeared you wanted no part of it. Now, not only are you suddenly interested in it, you come up with the wonderful idea of the field trip and offer to go along as a chaperone. Why the change?"

"Oh, it's not the project I object to. I just want to make sure the story they tell is an accurate one."

Actually, Sam had more than one reason for his change of heart. For one, if the kids were going to do a play about the town, wouldn't it be a good idea to make sure they did as good a job of it as possible? Putting aside his reservations about the whole historical thing, a public presentation by the local kids would be a great way to promote the town, and he was always looking for ways to promote Gold Bluff.

Another reason for his sudden involvement, and far and above the most important one from his point of view, was that Eden McKenna was totally absorbed with the project. If he hoped to spend any time at all with her, the best way to do it would be to join her rather than try to stop her.

Stop Eden McKenna when she'd set her mind on something? What a hoot *that* was! Oh, she looked harmless enough when you first met her. Lovely, adorable, and so darned sexy she could drive a man crazy just by looking at him.

So, after he'd realized old Tom was not about to let go of his desire to see the entire town used as a means to immortalize his family, a family Sam wasn't even sure actually existed, he'd decided he'd been going about things all wrong. He needed to work from the inside. Heck, if he had his way, he would become her right hand man. Her only man!

He could barely hold back a satisfied grin when he contemplated how it would be, working at her side. If she needed a tool, he'd be there. If she needed money, he'd get it for her. If she needed loving—ah, yes, he would most definitely be her go to guy.

And so he had come up with the idea of the senior campout. They would spend the entire weekend, getting to the ranch Friday afternoon and packing it in late Sunday afternoon. It was his idea that they would work together in small groups, each gathering information about various parts of the ranch. The groups would study each segment of the ranch, then make a group report of what they'd learned.

"It seems kind of repetitious for each group to cover the same ground," Eden had said when he first came up with the idea. "Wouldn't it be better if each group was assigned a different area to study?"

"That would be one way to do it, and maybe it would work out fine. I just thought it would be kind of interesting, as a sort of learning tool, to see what different perspectives came out of the different groups. Then, after they've gathered all the data they can, absorbed the 'feel' of the place, they can compare notes, maybe come up with a richer textured script."

"What a great idea! Are you sure you never thought about teaching? You have wonderful instincts."

"I think one teacher in the family will be enough," he said, then realized what he'd said. She just looked at him, a slightly puzzled expression on her face.

"My grandmother! Um, yeah. I never mentioned that I had a grandmother who used to teach, did I?"

"No, Sam, you never did," she smiled at his reddened face. "Funny you forgot to mention that before."

The following Saturday, thirteen students joined Eden and Sam on the trip out to the old Wenton ranch. Several of the students were able to drive their own cars, so, even though they were all loaded down with camping gear and enough food to satisfy the kids' hearty appetites, they were able to make the trip with only two other adults along to act as chaperones.

Although the ranch was only a few miles from town, many of the kids had never seen it before. Deep in the forest, it was in an area that would normally not have been of any real interest to them. After all, who cared about a bunch of falling down old buildings? But now that they had learned so much about the people who had once inhabited the ranch it had suddenly come alive to them.

"Ms. McKenna, is old Tom going to come out and give us a tour?" one of the boys asked. "He must know a whole lot about this old place."

"No, son, Tom Wenton has decided it would be best if you kids came up with your own impressions," Sam answered for Eden.

Actually, Tom had had every intention of spending the entire weekend with the kids—that was until Sam had set him straight. Surprisingly, Tom's best friend, Uncle Billy, had come to Sam's defense.

"Let the kids be," Billy had told Tom. "You already told them everything you remember about the old place. You want to get out there and try to corral all those wild kids? You think you have that much energy?"

In the end, Tom Wenton let someone besides himself run the show. Sam should have been pleased, but, frankly, it scared him half to death. What was Tom planning now, he wondered?

If Sam had thought he'd get Eden alone during the weekend, he quickly learned he'd been mistaken. Being the professional that she was, she maintained her position as teacher for the entire weekend. As far as he could tell, she never even considered compromising her responsibilities.

He would have been pleased, however, had he known that she was not above harboring some very romantic thoughts about her new assistant. He couldn't have known how pleased she was as she watched him helping the boys set up tents. Or when he worked so hard to get a campfire going that first night, only to have it turn into a dismal failure, giving off far more smoke than it did heat. It had taken two of the girls, both of whom had been Girl Scouts for several years, to get a really good fire going. But he'd tried, and that was what she noticed. And, no matter how bad the food had turned out, or how cold the night got, Sam Gorton was the consummate gentleman, never complaining, always ready to help out.

But when the campfire's flames began to dim, when the night became so dark you could barely make out the trees at the edge of the encampment, Sam displayed his greatest skill—that of camp ghost story teller extraordinaire. He had the girls squealing with delight and the boys demonstrating phony bravado by the time he'd finished with his goriest tale. Eden was fairly certain she needn't worry about any of the kids wanting to wander off into the darkness, which was what most concerned her. Not one soul who had listened to his tales would have even considered such foolishness. She wondered if that had been Sam's intention all along.

Both days were filled with discovery and new insights. The students spent hours in the barn, sifting through years of dirt and debris, finding several artifacts from the previous inhabitants. The old bunkhouse turned up even more relics of days gone by, an old boot, several hand-blown bottles, which had most likely contained beer or some other alcoholic beverage. There were even a couple of old tin cans, one for smoked oysters, the other for canned peaches.

Not much was left to find in the old house, but Eden had brought along the journal so she could read from it in the light of the campfire the second night while it still burned brightly.

"I can't imagine coming out here as a new bride," one of the girls said when Eden stopped reading the journal for a moment. "Just think how lonely it must have been."

"Yeah, way out here and there wasn't even a town nearby then."

"Well, there was the Indian village, down there at the end of the valley."

"I'd think that would have made it worse. It would have been scary living that close to Indians."

"But that tribe of Indians was friendly, at least it said so in the journal."

"Yeah, but she didn't know that when she first came here, did she? And she wasn't even as old as some of us are either. How would you like to do what she did when you were only sixteen years old? Personally, I think she was a real hero."

"So what about her old man? If she was a hero, so was he!" One of the boys voiced his opinion.

"Old man is right! Can you imagine? Tom's grandfather was thirty years old when he married Abbie. If you ask me, that's gross!"

Eden loved the way the kids were getting into the story of the Wenton's. By learning about this one pioneer family, they were learning so much about their own history. What better way could she have found to educate these kids about what life had been for those who had come before?

On Sunday morning the kids were far more subdued than they had been when they'd first arrived the morning before. They went about their work, sifting through piles of dirt and rubble, walking fence lines, sometimes just gazing at the old buildings, seeing in their minds' eyes the life that had gone on there so many years before.

When it came time for them to leave, there was very little chatter. It was as if they all felt a kinship for the old farm and its inhabitants, though they had met them only in their imaginations.

"You know, Ms. McKenna, I'd started writing notes on how I thought the play should go," one of the girls told Eden in class the next morning. "But after I got home last night I threw them all in the trash. I'd thought the play should be all about the gold mine. But now, after going out there and all, I think it should be about Abigail Wenton more than the gold."

"But she's the one who found the gold. We can't just forget about that, can we?

"That's not actually true, Todd. She didn't find the gold, the Indians did. But, yes, it was she who turned it into a mine. I certainly don't think we should forget about the gold. All I meant was it's the people who count. They count a whole lot more than a bunch of gold."

Eden couldn't have been more pleased.

"Yes, Leslie, and if you learn nothing more about history in this class, you will have learned the most important thing of all. All history is, is a bunch of stories about people. What people did, how they lived, and how they thought. And all of this is what makes our civilization what it is—for better or for worse."

Chapter Nine

"So, how's the epic coming along?"

She glanced up from the pile of papers that nearly covered her desk and was pleased to see both Tom and Billy standing in the doorway. "Overwhelming!" she said, indicating the papers she had been busy grading. "Come on in and take a look at some of these papers. I can't believe the work some of these kids are producing. I knew I had some very bright students, but I certainly never expected to see work such as this."

"So, do you have enough material for your play?" Billy asked as he glanced with obvious interest at the stacks of papers.

She looked at him for a moment as she gave his question her serious consideration. Then, lifting one paper and then another, she said, "What we have here is wonderful. They've really done so well with the material."

"But…? Something tells me you aren't completely satisfied." Tom noted.

She looked up from the papers, nodding her head reflectively.

"What I'm looking at here is a first act," she said, lifting her eyebrows in a what-can-I-say expression. "They've worked so darned hard, I don't know how I'm going to go back to them and tell them they're only about half way through with their research. Especially when they've all been telling me that all they seem to be able to dig up about this area isn't really about the town of Gold Bluff, but rather the earlier history of the region."

"You mean the story about the Wenton family isn't enough?"

She couldn't help but note the tone of disappointment in Tom's voice.

"Oh, it could be enough, that is, if the kids will be satisfied with just a one act play. But after seeing their enthusiasm for this project, I'm afraid they're going to feel cheated if we don't go for a full production, which would mean the play will have to have at least two acts—if not three."

Tom began pacing, glancing out the window, tracing his fingers along one of the desks, obviously stalling for time while he did a little thinking. Eden watched him, wondering what could possibly be going on in his head. Obviously something was playing very heavily on his mind. He finally stopped pacing and turned to face her once again.

"I may be able to help you," he said, his expression indicating he wasn't at all certain he was doing the right thing. "I guess it's time I brought out the big guns."

Billy's usual humorous expression sobered immediately.

"You aren't going to…?"

Tom did not give him a chance to finish whatever it was he was about to say. "It's time I showed her the Stossard house."

"You mean that beautiful old mansion on the outskirts of town?"

"Yes, ma'am, that's the one. The old Mayor's Mansion, that's what the town always used to call it," Billy affirmed.

"Is it true no one lives there now? I've heard the kids say the place is haunted."

"Well if it isn't, it should be. But I don't rightfully think it is. It's just old, filled with a lot of old things, some of which are probably better left forgotten."

"Do you know who owns it? Do you think you could get us inside?"

"Being as I *am* the owner, I'd judge getting us in won't be a problem. If you're interested, I could take you there right now."

"Interested! Just try to keep me away."

Too excited to grade one more paper, she stuffed them all into her attaché case, grabbed her purse and was out the door before Tom had a chance to change his mind.

*****

Tom's reluctance to enter the building was unmistakable. He stood at the front gate, his hand resting on the old iron fence, a troubled expression in his tired old eyes.

"Tom? Are you sure you want to go through with this? We could do it some other time. Heck, there's nothing saying we *have* to put on more than a one act play."

"No, I want the whole story told."

He spoke in a tone she'd never heard from him before.

"He hasn't been in the place since his Aunt Ruth died in it."

"Oh, Tom, are you sure you want to share the house with me? What memories it must contain for you."

"Oh, he's got memories in there, all right," Billy observed wryly.

"The Aunt Ruth who lived here, would that be the same Ruth mentioned in your mother's journal?" Eden asked as she turned her gaze back to the house, "the one who married the man who eventually became the town's mayor?"

"That's Aunt Ruth, all right.

"My goodness, I can't believe we're actually going to see where she lived. Although I realize it won't be like it was when she lived here. I'm sure others must have lived in it since then, and put their own print on it. But still, the idea that we'll be trodding the same floors she walked on… What a thrill this will be."

"Here, you go on in." Tom reached into his pocket and pulled out a huge key. "I'll join you in a minute."

"Are you sure you want to do this?" she asked. She

couldn't ignore the tightness she heard in the old man's voice. "If this is going to cause you pain it simply isn't worth it."

"No, no, you go on in. I've waited longer'n I should'a."

"You go on, now," Uncle Billy spoke up. "This is something Tom's needed to do for a long time. We'll be in in just a minute or two."

Tom waited until Eden had entered the house before he turned his attention to his friend.

"You sure you took care of everything?" Tom asked under his breath.

"If you didn't trust me to do the job, then why the heck did you give it to me?"

"I trust you, it's just that it's so danged important she finds that stuff. You sure you put those boxes where she can't miss them?"

"Look, if Eden doesn't find them then she's not the woman I think she is."

"You didn't go and make it too obvious, did you?"

"Dang, will you stop worrying? She'll find them, and where she finds them will be exactly where she'll be expecting to find stuff like that."

Billy couldn't remember ever seeing Tom act like this. If he didn't know his old friend better, he'd actually believe his act about the house holding so many memories.

"You going to be all right about this?" For once there was no teasing in Billy's voice, just concern.

"Yeah. Well, no, actually, as a matter of fact, I'm not all right about it at all. But it's something that needs to be done. But no matter what we find in there, if there's secrets to be discovered, I figure I'd rather have them found by someone like little Eden than anyone else. They'd a been found eventually, better it be by a nice lady like her."

"Maybe there's nothing in there to find. You don't know for a fact your uncle was the one who started that fire. And even if he was, there's no reason to figure there'd be anything left behind to pin the blame on him."

"Aunt Ruth kept a journal of everything that went on in town, as well as in her own life. It was almost like a religion with the woman. I doubt that a day went by without her chronicling the day's events. I can't imagine her not writing about what happened that day."

There was a sadness in Tom's eyes when he finished speaking, as if the thought of his aunt having to endure years of self-inflicted isolation was about to break his heart. He was still for a moment, then said, "She was a good woman. She shouldn't have had to go through all that."

The silence that had settled over the two old men was finally broken by Billy.

"Well, are you ready to face the music, or do you plan on standing out here all day?" he goaded, knowing that was just the thing his old friend needed. A gentle hand would have done more harm than good

*****

"Tom! Billy! Look at all this! Tell me I'm not dreaming that all of this is original."

From the moment Eden entered the house she felt transported to another time, a time of corsets and calling cards; a time when a lady's most important duty was to oversee the running of her home. Not to do the actual work, mind you. If that were the case she would hardly be a lady, now would she?

"If by original you mean, did it all belong to my aunt, then yes, it's the original stuff, all right."

"This is too fantastic! Why, it's as if history has been frozen right here in these rooms!" She ran from one room to another, her enthusiasm building with each step. Amused, the two old men followed behind.

The rooms reflected the tastes of a Victorian woman who had been gifted with enough funds to indulge her every whim. The overly decorated rooms would have suffocated another person who was not as fascinated by the past as Eden was. Richly colored oriental rugs covered the floors, the hallways, even the wide stairs that led to the second floor. Tufted velvet furniture, in hues that reflected the many colors of the carpets, filled the rooms.

The velvet brocade wall coverings were so richly colored they should have dominated the rooms, yet, because of the many paintings and framed objects, the eye barely noticed their richness. Eden stood in the formal parlor, her gaze shifting eagerly from one gorgeous painting to another, from a grouping of mounted butterflies to the ornately framed black silhouette of a young boy.

As she gazed at the silhouette she felt Tom's approach.

"Do you have any idea who this adorable child was?" she glanced over her shoulder at him. "Wasn't he just the cutest thing you ever saw?"

"Oh, I was a cutey back then," Tom grinned self-consciously.

"No! You? I don't believe it!"

"You're not the only one," Uncle Billy mumbled from across the room.

She stepped from the parlor to the music room, then into the dining room. It was huge, larger by far than the living room in her tiny house. Sixteen chairs stood sentinel around the long table. An elaborately embellished silver urn, black with years of tarnish, graced its center. Against the longest wall stood a matching sideboard still filled with more silver pieces in a pattern that matched the urn.

Behind the dining room there was a butler's pantry, its shelves still laden with a twenty-four place settings of Havilland china. Crystal stemware of every size and use was housed behind glass cupboard doors.

The kitchen was a history teacher's delight, filled as it was with not one single modern appliance. How she would love to see a meal being prepared in this room, she thought. To feel the heat of the coal stove, to smell the scents of freshly grown vegetables as they simmered in one of those huge iron kettles.

Leaving the kitchen behind, Tom led her up the stairs, which took three turns before ending up at the second story.

"I think you might find this room interesting," he said as he opened the door to the first room they came to. "This was my aunt's own room and that little alcove over there, that's where she handled her correspondence."

Eden stepped reverently through the door. Everything in the room was exactly as it would be if someone were still living in the house. The bed was made, covered with a delicately crocheted coverlet. Opening the closets she noted they were still filled with a woman's dresses. She could barely breath she was so thrilled with discovery.

Closing the wardrobe door, she made her way around the room, touching first one object and then another. Her eyes misted with the realization that a real live woman had once occupied these rooms, a woman who had for some reason left everything she owned behind when she left.

"What happened?" she asked. "Why are all her things still here? I mean, surely she's been dead for a very long time. You would think that someone would have cleared the house out long ago."

"There was something of a mystery about my Aunt Ruth. It was something that happened to the town—something bad. To this day the mystery's never been solved. I was kind'a hoping you'd be able to help Billy and me figure out what happened."

"Me? Oh, Tom, I think you've vastly overestimated me. I wouldn't have the foggiest notion of how to go about solving a mystery."

"Maybe you do and maybe you don't. The way Tom and I figure it, if you haven't ever tried something, then, heck, you don't know if you can do it or not, do you?"

"I don't expect you to make a commitment about this, not yet anyway. Why don't you go on checking out the old place? Who knows, maybe you'll find something stashed away somewhere that can give the kid's play what it needs.

Eden knew she was way out of her league, but her curiosity could not be contained. Smiling absentmindedly at the two men, she turned back to her search, walking into the alcove where the old woman had conducted her personal business.

"Over here, just look! Oh, my-gosh I can't believe my eyes," her voice was suddenly filled with awe. "This is it! This may be just what I've been looking for!"

"You mean you've found a clue to my aunt's secret?" Tom's voice was filled with astonishment. "I thought you might be a big help, but I sure didn't think you'd find anything this fast."

"Oh, Tom, I'm sorry. I didn't mean to let you think that. No, what I found was this box of old photos. And look, there's another box filled with old receipts and other business papers. This whole room is a treasure trove of historical data. I wouldn't be a bit surprised to learn that the entire town's history can be traced through these old photos."

Chapter Ten

Hey! Let me help you with those."

Eden heard Sam's voice coming from behind her. Stepping away from her car, she stood upright, reaching back with both hands to massage the small of her back.

"Sam Gorton, you are my knight in shining armor. Tell me, is carrying boxes for lady teachers listed on the job description for the city's mayor?"

"That it is, along with mowing her lawn and pruning her rose bushes." He grinned at her as he reached down to lift one of the several boxes she'd brought from the Stossard Mansion.

"I heard you've dropped off the School Board completely. I thought you liked your new position."

"I liked it okay, but I decided it might be a good idea if I was to get off the Board completely."

"When did that happen? And, if you don't mind my asking, why?" They continued talking as they unloaded the boxes from Eden's car and carried them into her house.

"I can easily answer the 'when' part of your question. That answer is at about two o'clock this afternoon. The 'why' part, well, let's just say I wanted to avoid any possible conflicts of interest."

She wasn't entirely sure how she felt about this new development. When he'd stepped down as the head of the board so he would be free to date her, she had to admit she'd been flattered. He'd made it fairly obvious he didn't want the fact that she reported directly to him to get in the way of their blossoming friendship. But, even though he was no longer the head of the School Board he was still part of management which she felt still put a barrier between them. What she wasn't certain about was if she had subconsciously relied on that barrier to help her keep their relationship on a platonic level. She wasn't sure how she felt about that barrier being lifted.

It seemed as if she had spent her entire adult life playing it safe when it came to entering into a close relationship with a man. It had been the easy thing to. So easy, in fact, that she rarely even considered changing her ways.

She was a smart woman, smart enough to notice the pain her friends suffered after the breakup of a relationship. She'd seen enough of her friends' tears to convince her to keep her heart locked up safely.

That was before she had met Sam Gorton. She couldn't deny she was attracted to him. But was she ready to let a man into her life?

"I'd rather hoped you would be able to guess why I choose to no longer be your boss or even remotely connected to your boss," Sam replied, his voice lowering to a more intimate tone.

"Sometimes it's not the best idea to try to guess what another person is thinking. Guessing can get you in a whole lot of trouble."

Sam didn't comment on her observation directly, but chose instead to find a spot on the already crowded dining room table on which to place the last of the boxes of photos he had removed from her car. Relieved of his burden, he turned to her, a delightfully wicked smile shining from his eyes. Without saying a word, he closed the small distance that separated them. Taking her into his arms, he captured her mouth with his. If she had any doubts about his intentions, they were quickly erased.

The kiss they had shared on the train had been a sweet, public sort of kiss, one that made a person long for more yet be happy that the "more" was not performed in front of others. Their second kiss, while more private, had still occurred in a place too public to allow for a great deal of intimacy. This kiss, however, was one that most definitely required a private place, preferably a private place where they would not be interrupted.

His arms pulled her to him in a gentle yet seductive move, giving her every opportunity to pull away if she chose. But pulling away never entered her mind. When his lips joined hers she marveled that no others had ever felt so perfect. Their lips fit together like pieces of a jigsaw puzzle, as if they had been manufactured from the same material and had finally found their mates.

Just when she thought she might die of pure joy, he stepped back, releasing her. She gazed up at him with misted eyes. She felt herself smiling like a blithering idiot, but couldn't seem to stop. She would have felt the complete and utter fool if he had not been looking at her with the exact same expression on his face.

"I think you made a wise decision," was all she could think to say.

"I was hoping you'd feel that way," he said as he once more reached out for her, pulling her into his arms for another soul searching kiss.

He knew better than to let his emotions get away from him, yet how was he to do that when everything he'd ever wanted in a woman was right there in his arms? He tried to keep his hunger for her at bay, but it was awfully difficult to do it when she clung to him like that. As the kiss deepened, their mutual needs taking over what good intentions they might have had, they pulled closer, then closer still, until their bodies seemed to form a single unit.

Warm, liquid sensations raced through his body as he felt the tip of her tongue darting tentatively against his lips. Never one to deny a lady, he responded by opening his mouth to welcome her delightful invasion. As he twined his tongue around hers, tasting her sweetness, he felt himself respond to her in a most ungentlemanly manner. Oh, good Lord, he was going to ruin everything, he thought as he tried to shift his body in such a way that his need would not be quite so obvious.

*****

Things were happening to Eden that had never happened before. She had no thoughts, just sensations—wonderful, delightful sensations. She let her tongue play with his, savoring the taste of him. Her entire body had become a raging flame of passion. As the kiss lengthened and she felt his need press against her, the flames that raced through her body raged on, building in intensity until she thought she'd die if it didn't stop.

*****

As much as he regretted it, Sam finally came to the realization that if he didn't break the kiss soon they would both most likely pass out from lack of oxygen. Though he hated to do it, he forced himself to pull away. Breathing deeply, he rested his chin on the top of her head, a position which directed his eyes into the most dangerous room in the house—Eden's bedroom.

The temptation to pick her up in his arms and carry her to that tempting oasis was nearly overpowering. His overactive imagination supplied enticing erotic images of the delights they could sample together there. He quickly shut his eyes, directing his mind away from the temptation. Good Lord, if she knew what he was thinking she'd probably have him out the front door and onto the street before he knew what had hit him. Releasing his hold on her, he stepped back, away from temptation.

What she did next was his complete undoing. Without saying a word, she reached up and began undoing the buttons on his shirt.

*****

She felt the complete wanton, but knew if she didn't do something very quickly this perfect moment would be gone. She couldn't let that happen. With trembling fingers, she slowly, yet very methodically, began to undress him. As she released the buttons on his shirt, she let her hands slide over his chest, glorying in the tense muscles, the heated flesh.

Unable, or unwilling, to stop herself, she dusted his chest with light kisses. The touching and the kissing were not enough. A craving built up in her, driving her on. She reached out to him with the very tip of her tongue, tracing where her fingers had touched just moments before. When she heard the sharp intake of his breath, she looked up into his eyes, praying she would see a need that matched her own. She was not disappointed.

It was all she needed. Taking his hand, she turned toward her bedroom. Walking with slow, very deliberate steps, she looked back over her shoulder, smiling up into his eyes. She saw a question there, but smiled it away.

She had no questions now, but she did have an answer. And that answer was to be found in only one place—on her beautiful Victorian bed.

*****

They lay snuggled together, her cute little bottom snuggled tight against his now satisfied manhood. He could feel his heartbeat slowing, knowing that the beat of her heart matched his own. He'd never known such contentment, or such awe.

He felt himself drifting off to sleep and simply let it happen. It felt so natural being in Eden's bed, sleeping with her in his arms, feeling the warmth of her breath brush against the hairs on his arm as she slumbered. It wasn't until he was on the very edge of consciousness that a question suddenly popped into his mind. What was in those boxes he'd carried in for her?

*****

"Boxes?" Eden asked in a sleepy voice. She'd woken only moments before to the smell of freshly brewed coffee drifting in from the kitchen. It took her a second to get her brain to work. "Oh! You mean *those* boxes. They're just some things I brought back from the Stossard Mansion."

Wrapping a sheet around herself in a sudden fit of

modesty, Eden padded barefoot across the bedroom to retrieve her comfortable old bathrobe. Slipping into the robe and tying it firmly at the waist, she joined Sam in her living room where he was looking with curiosity at the boxes in question.

"What? You've been out there? I figured that old place would have been totally emptied out long ago. It's been abandoned for as long as I can remember."

"Oh, it's far from abandoned. As you probably already know, it once belonged to Tom Wenton's aunt, the one who was married to the town's first mayor. When she died she left it and everything in it to Tom and, for some reason, he hasn't ever been able to bring himself to do anything with it."

As she spoke about the house, Eden stepped over to the boxes and began lifting out old photos. Her fascination with the boxes' contents kept her from noting the strained expression that spread over Sam's face.

"He told you all that, did he?" Sam asked, his voice suddenly strained.

"He not only told me about it, he took me on a guided tour of the entire house, from basement to attic. Oh, Sam, you can't imagine the treasures that old house contains. Why, the house itself is a museum."

Sam could barely control the groan he felt bubbling up from deep within himself. Would Tom never cease causing trouble?

"Come over here and look at these old photos. Why, I bet if we laid them out properly, we could get a complete picture of what Gold Bluff looked like all those years ago." She began pulling out more of the photos, looking at the back of them, hoping to find something written there that would tell her where in the city the various dwellings belonged.

"This will make a wonderful project for my students, don't you think?"

"What? Project? Oh, right… your students. Yeah, that would be good." Sam knew he was acting like a total fool, but he couldn't help himself. What the heck had Tom Wenton done now?

"Goodness! Look at the time!" he blurted out, grasping at anything that would help him make a somewhat reasonable exit. "I've got to go… I mean, I… That is… it's just that I was supposed to meet a client fifteen minutes ago. They want to buy a house, well, a business actually…"

She turned a bemused smile at him. "Mustn't hold up business then. Maybe you can come by later. We could begin sorting out these pictures."

"Oh, I don't know… about the pictures, I mean. I never was much good at things like that. But about my coming by later, of course I'll be back. I mean, I'd like nothing better than seeing you again…you and I… but the pictures…"

"Sam Gorton, if I didn't know you better, I'd say you were blushing!"

"Well…"

"Look, Sam, what just happened between us, it's more important than any pictures. It was very…well…"

"Lady, if you can't count on anything else in this entire universe, you can rest assured that what happened between us today was way beyond important."

*****

She was pleased to see his self-esteem had returned full force. Though she found the stammering, shy side of him to be charming, she was relieved to see the self-assured, even cocky, Sam she'd come to know returned to her. How many more sides of Sam Gorton were there, she wondered? Had she just scratched the surface of a very complex man?

*****

"Ms. McKenna, would you mind coming over here?" Johnny Wilson called out to her from across the room. The Town Site committee, a group of kids who had volunteered to study the photos and place them in the relative order of where the various buildings now stood, had placed two large classroom tables end-to-end for the project. Because the town rested in a long, narrow canyon, the pictures nearly covered the entire length of the tables.

"Making any headway?" Eden asked as she peered over her students' shoulders.

"I don't know, Ms. McKenna. Most of the old buildings in the photos look like places here in town, but when we try putting them where they belong, they don't all fit right."

"How do you mean?" Eden leaned closer to the pictures.

"Well, look over here," Todd Hampton pointed to one end of the table. "Over here we have what looks like an old blacksmith store. We know it belongs here because of that boulder there. I mean, you can't mistake that huge thing, right?"

"Right, if I remember correctly, that's the boulder that marks the corner of Riverside Road and Black Bear Street."

"Exactly! But instead of the old blacksmith store being there now, there's a two story house."

"True, but there's nothing saying the blacksmith store wasn't torn down after automobiles came in and was replaced by the house that's there now."

"Nothing, except that here's a picture of that very same house. And, as you can see, there is definitely no boulder anywhere near the house in this picture." Janie held up another of the photos for Eden to see.

Eden took the picture the girl was holding out to her. The kids were right, it did look just like the house that now stood by the boulder—in the exact spot where the old blacksmith shop must have stood over a century ago.

"This house does have a striking resemblance to the

house that stands on that lot," she conceded.

"Not just a resemblance, Ms. McKenna. I live just a couple of houses down the street from that place, and I'm here to tell you, it's the exact same house. I mean, there's been some work done to it, paint and stuff like that, but the house itself, it's the very same one."

"I suppose it could have been moved from one lot to another." Eden's voice echoed her doubt to that theory. The house was fairly large. It would have taken a major effort to have moved it from one lot to another. Why would anyone have wanted to go to so much trouble? Still, it could have been done. Yes, that must be the answer.

"But that's not all," another of the students commented. "Take a look at this picture of the Methodist church. See that mountain peak? The one there on the right side of the picture?"

Eden gazed at the photo. Sure enough, there in plain sight was a very distinctive mountain peak.

"That's Eagle Mountain. If you want to see Eagle Mountain from the Methodist church, you have to stand facing *away* from the church, not toward it. At least that's the way it is these days."

"Are you sure?" Eden asked, a frown creasing her brow.

"Yes, ma'am. My family goes to that church. Every time I come out from service, I always enjoy the view of Eagle Mountain as I walk down the steps."

"You know? I could accept someone wanting to move a house from one spot to another," one of the boys spoke up, "even though I can't think of why they'd want to bother. But turning a church around? Now, that's one I'm not buying."

"It does seem odd, doesn't it?" Eden had to admit this was all very confusing. "I think I'd better ask Mr. Wenton to look at what we've got here. Maybe he can shed some light on this mystery."

*****

"There's no mystery here," Tom spoke jovially to Eden later that afternoon after her students had departed for the day. "You got to figure in the fire."

"Oh, right, you did mention there having been a fire in Gold Bluff. But from what you said, I didn't think there was much to it," Eden said.

"It was a humdinger of a fire! Heck, these old towns, they were always burning down. Why do you think the volunteer fire departments were so popular back in those days?"

"I realize fire was a constant hazard in these towns, considering that almost everything was built of wood. But still and all, I didn't figure too much of the town was involved."

"An oversight, just an oversight."

"This is going to be a bigger job than I'd figured on. Just how big was this fire, anyway?"

"Oh, it was big, all right. *Really*, big."

"Can you give me some idea of its boundaries?"

"Um, boundaries..." For the first time since she'd known him, old Tom seemed at a loss for words. If she was not mistaken, he had a very definite bad-boy-caught-with-his-hand-in-the-apple-basket expression on his face.

"Yes, boundaries. You do know which part of the town still consists of original buildings, don't you?"

Tom hesitated for a moment before answering. The look on his face gave her a very uncomfortable feeling. What the heck was he trying to hide, anyway?

"How big was the fire, Tom? How many buildings burnt down?"

"Most of 'em," he mumbled.

"Most of them, you say. I see."

She pulled out a nearby chair and lowered herself into it. The sinking feeling in her stomach threatened to affect her legs and she wasn't too sure how long they would support her.

"How much of the town was left standing after the fire?" She wasn't even sure if she wanted to know the answer, but knew in her heart she couldn't ignore her responsibility of getting all the historical facts straight.

Sighing deeply, Tom answered. "The only place left was my aunt's house, the Stossard Mansion."

He pulled out another chair and lowered himself into it. He faced himself away from Eden, keeping his eyes on the hundreds of photos that lay scattered across the table.

"So, the town's history… how much of it's true?" she finally forced herself to ask.

"Most of it. That is, all these houses, we rebuilt each and every one of them just like they were back when my family settled these parts."

"They're all replicas is what you're telling me? All made to appear original?"

"Right! They're all, each and every one of them, built to replace the ones that were here originally."

"But, Tom, they aren't the originals that people thought they were buying. The entire population of Gold Bluff bought into a deception."

"That's not true! These houses, this town … it's just exactly the way it was back then… only newer."

Eden's only answer was a shake of her head and a groan. The old man simply did not get it. He, along with the town's so called leaders, all of them, even Sam, had deceived every single resident in this "perfect" city. Now that she knew the truth, what the heck was she supposed to do about it?

And even more important to her personally; how could she reconcile her feelings for a man who she knew had deceived not only her but hundreds of others—all for the sake of making a profit.

Damn, this was so not like the man she had come to

know Sam Gorton to be. The lies and deceptions were things she might have expected of Sam before she'd come to know the real man. The Sam who would have pulled off this scheme was nothing like the man she had come care for, to respect.

Okay, hell, she might as well go ahead and admit it, Sam was the first man she had ever let touch her heart. He was the first man who she had allowed herself to love. He was the only man she had truly believed in, lock, stock and barrel.

Now she realized that she couldn't have been a bigger fool. As far as she was concerned, the man who had interviewed her, the man who represented a profession she believed consisted of the lowest form of life, was exactly what she had first envisioned him to be, someone who would never think twice about scamming poor, innocent people…people who trusted him…people whose lives might be shattered when they learned the full extent of what he and his partners had done.

Chapter Eleven

"Well, it finally happened! I told you guys it would, but nobody would listen."

Sam's distraught facial expression left no doubt as to how he was feeling as he lowered himself into the chair nearest to him. He and the rest of the partners had met after business hours, in the privacy of the bank's conference room where they could be certain they would have privacy.

"You guys said I worried too much, that if I wasn't so interested in Eden, I'd realize there wasn't anything to be concerned about," he continued. "Well, I'd say we've all got something to worry about now."

All of the stock holders in the Gold Bluff Investment Group sat around the bank's executive conference table, the atmosphere as thick as a San Francisco fog bank.

"What I'd like to know is, what the heck you were thinking letting her get her hands on those old photos, Tom? Were you trying to sabotage us?" George Bryant, the banker, asked, his face beet red with anger.

"I had my reasons," Tom replied, his steady gaze and firmly set jaw telling his companions he did not intend to back down one step.

"I don't suppose you'd care to let us in on those reasons," Mason Bloomington spoke up.

"No, I can't say as I would, beyond saying it was something that needed doing, so I did it."

Several of the men who were gathered around the table groaned aloud at Tom's statement. George voiced what several of the others were thinking when he asked, "Billy, were you in on this with Tom?"

"If you mean, was I there when he gave Eden the photos, then the answer is yes. I was there and, as far as I'm concerned, Tom did exactly what he should've."

"But, why? Don't you two realize what this means? We could all be sued, you old fools!"

"Maybe we will be, and maybe we won't. And maybe it's about time we shed a little light on what's been going on around here."

"Which is?" Joe Stanton asked belligerently. .

"That you've been so all fired caught up in selling a story you don't believe in yourselves that you're scared shitless someone will find out you're lying. And, if you ask me, that's no way to live!" Tom shouted back.

"Who the hell do you think you are to point fingers at us? You're in this as deep as any of the rest of us!"

"Not the way Billy and I see it, we aren't, are we Billy?"

"Not from where I stand. You guys are so worried the truth will come out. We figure it's about time it did."

"I don't know, maybe things aren't a bad as they seem," Mason spoke up. "We sold houses to people who believed they were buying part of California's gold rush history, which in a way was the truth; just not exactly the whole truth.

"But we did sell those houses under false pretenses. We never happened to mention that every single one of those buildings was a replica, not the real thing." George observed.

"We can't let that ruin everything we've built here. We all stand to lose too much."

Sam remained silent while his partners sparred with one another. The more the men argued, the lower he slumped in his chair. The whole bunch of them could yell all day about what they stood to lose, but there wasn't one of them that stood to lose as much as he already had. All they would lose was money. His loss went so far beyond mere money he could barely bring himself to face it. For in his heart he knew he had lost the greatest treasure he would ever know—the hope of gaining Eden's love and respect.

"Okay, okay," he said finally as he pulled himself to a standing position. "What's been done is done. What we need to talk about now is what we're going to do about it."

Another loud burst of conversation erupted around the table. With everyone talking at once, no one voice stood out from the others. The turmoil continued for several moments, until the noise finally died down when they all began to realize that no one was listening to any of the others. With one or two final mumbled comments, a silence finally settled over the room.

"Sam's right," Mason spoke up from the end of the table. "What we need to do is get a spin on this thing. Hell, with a little tweaking here and there, we ought to be able to come up with something that will pull this out of the fire."

"Right! We can do this, guys," George agreed. "All we have to do is come up with the right story!"

"Wrong! Haven't you guys learned anything? Our fancy story is what got us into this problem in the first place. Another one will only get us in deeper. There's only one way we can deal with this and that's to come clean. It's time we did the right thing. We've got to tell the truth."

Sam looked from one man to another. On some faces there was open hostility, on others confusion. There was, however, no hostility *or* confusion reflected in the two oldest members, Tom and Billy. What he saw on their faces was a mixture of relief and satisfaction.

"What do we do now, Sam?" Joe Stanton asked.

Sam was relieved to note that the expression on his friend's face now matched the two older men. He felt a huge sense of relief that, with four members of the partnership agreeing to go public with the truth, the other three would have to go along with the majority.

"There's only one thing we can do. We call a town meeting."

*****

Eden sat in her living room with the cat she had

acquired soon after moving to Gold Bluff and a cup of tea. Stroking Buster's sleek coat, she let her gaze wander around the room. She'd loved this house from the first moment she had seen it. Now she wasn't sure what she felt about it. How much had it meant to her that the house was over a hundred years old? Was it the history of it she loved, or the house itself?

Looking around the room, she had to admit that everything about it remained the same. It was just as cozy as it had been before she'd learned it was a replica of the original. She still had that "at home" feeling when she stepped through the front door. Her belongings still looked as if they'd found the home they had been made for. The only thing that had changed about the house was her perception of it. Just how important was that perception?

And how important was it that the entire town of Gold Bluff was built on nothing more than lies? That the buildings the townspeople had bought believing they were actual historical treasures were merely replicas of the originals? Was it her responsibility to set the record straight? Would the other residents want to know the truth? Or would it only muddy the waters? This was such a great place to live. Would her revelation help or hurt its residents?

But as confusing as all of this was, none of it compared to her mixed feelings about Sam. Like her adorable house, Sam too had come to feel like a perfect fit for her. She'd never felt as comfortable with any man as she did with him. It was so easy to laugh with him...to talk...to dream.

But now she wondered if she had ever known the true Sam Gorton. Had he been leading her on as he had so many others? And even if he hadn't been, did she really want to be involved with someone who would have been part of the lies he and his partners had spread?

The answer to that question was all too clear,

although just thinking about it gave her a pain deep in her heart. The sweet promises of his kisses were empty. There could be no future for her with a man who chose lies over truth.

"Well, damn. Now what do I do?"

Unfortunately, she knew the answer to that question. She would have to leave Gold Bluff. Sure, she'd stay until the end of the school year; she owed that to the kids, if nothing else. But after that she was out of there.

But where to, she wondered? Back to San Francisco with its overcrowded classrooms and students who rarely bothered to listen to her? No, that life was gone forever. Though the life she'd known here had been built on a lie, she knew in her heart it had changed her forever. She would find a place for herself, no matter how long the search. If she'd learned but one thing in Gold Bluff, it was that she would never again settle for less than what her heart told her was right for her. But darn it anyway, if Gold Bluff and Sam weren't right for her, what was?

Since she'd been too much of a bookworm to find the time for close male/female relationships she had little experience in how a person went about putting an end to one. Although she and Sam had been seeing one another for several weeks now, the relationship hadn't gotten into the making promises stage as yet. Had they gotten to the stage where she had the right to storm over to his house and have it out with him? Did she even want that?

No, she definitely did *not* want to have a shouting match with Sam. That would mean losing her composure, and that was something she never did. Well, hardly ever. What she desperately wanted to do was to go over there and have him tell her it had all been a mistake. That he'd never lied to her. But that was just wishful thinking, and wasn't wishful thinking what had gotten her into this mess in the first place?

Hadn't she come here wishing for a fresh start? A

better life? And hadn't she given her heart to Sam because of a wish for a fuller, more complete life? A life with a husband, a couple of kids and a dog or two?

*****

After giving it a great deal of thought, Eden decided she would not go to Sam with her rage. She'd go to him with her sorrow.

She called him first, asking if he would meet her at his office, knowing Betty would have left for the day.

"I thought we had a date for dinner," Sam reminded her with a question in his voice.

"We did, but I'm afraid I'm going to have to back out. But I do need to talk to you, Sam. Could I come over right now?" He agreed to her request, but she could tell by the tone of his voice he was disturbed by the change of plans.

He was waiting for her in the outer office. When she stepped through the door, he opened the door to his private office, motioning to her to enter.

"We don't need to go in there. This will do just fine," she said as she stood before him, looking him straight in the eye.

"You lied to me." It was a statement, not a question.

Well, he'd known it was coming, hadn't he? When Tom told him about Eden's discovery Sam had known this moment was on its way. All the hoping and praying in the world would never change who Eden was and he knew it. Honesty was her bible, the truth her only standard. He'd let her down and now he was going to have to pay for it.

"Yes," was his reply, no more lies, no more excuses.

She walked over to the window nearest Betty's desk. Her back was to Sam as she stood looking out at the street.

"I'll be leaving at the end of the semester."

"Is this your formal notice? Because, if it is you

should give it to Joe, not me."

She turned away from the window and faced him directly as she said, "I suppose you might call this my 'informal' notice. I just thought you'd want to know, that's all."

"I don't suppose there's anything I can say to change your mind."

He wanted desperately to close the distance that separated them, to take her into his arms and pretend that none of this was happening. But he didn't. He simply stood there, gazing at her, trying to memorize everything about her before he lost her forever.

"No," she replied, her eyes reflecting the sadness in her heart. "I can't stay someplace that's built on lies, Sam. I can't stay here and pretend ignorance of what I discovered, this…this… Gold Bluff deception you and your partners have perpetrated. And I can't continue seeing someone who would do something like this."

"I see." Sam, the man with the glib tongue, the quick joke, had absolutely nothing to say. How could a man talk when he was completely hollow inside?

She stood there for a moment, looking at him as if she hoped he'd say something to make her unhappiness go away. Then, with eyes filled with heartbreaking sorrow, she turned from him and walked silently out the door and out of his life.

*****

"You noticed the way our love birds been acting lately?" Uncle Billy asked Tom as his eyes tracked Sam entering his office two days after Eden had confronted him about the deception. Once again the two old men sat on their bench outside the Mercantile, holding court over the town they both loved. "Sammy doesn't look too happy, does he?"

Tom peered across the street at the target of their conversation. He watched Sam trudge slowly up the steps then open his office door and step through. He waited until the door was shut, cutting off any further opportunity for the two of them to assess him before making his response.

"Seen him look better," was his cryptic reply.

"Wonder what's going on? You don't think Eden's giving him grief about what she found out, do you?"

"Knowing that girl, I wouldn't be a bit surprised. There's not a false bone in Eden McKenna's body and I don't suppose she'd take it too lightly that we all played so loose with the facts about Gold Bluff."

"But she wouldn't take it out on Sam, would she?"

"She's a woman, you old fool. Of course she'd take it out on him. He's the only one she really cares about. Do you think she'd waste her time cussing out a bunch of guys that don't mean a hill of beans to her?"

Since Uncle Billy had never been married, he accepted the sixty-five year married man's take on the situation.

"You think we ought to go over there and see if there's anything we can do? I mean, I'd sure hate to see anything come between them two."

Tom reached up to scratch his bristly chin as he pondered his answer to Billy's question.

"Well, I don't rightly know about that. A man like Sam, I expect he might not be too happy to see me right about now. Somehow he's got it in his head I had something to do with his problems. I can't imagine how he got that idea, but still and all…"

"Sam may have his ways about him, but I always liked the guy. I'd sure hate to see him lose out on something as important as being with Eden, if that's what makes him happy. I think we ought to go over there and see if there's anything we can do to help."

"Ah, Billy…" Tom squirmed uncomfortably on the old wooden bench. "I don't think…"

"That's right, old man, you don't think. Not as

much as you ought to, anyway. The way I see it, we had a lot to do with the way things are around here, you even more than me, and if there's anything we can do to make things right, well, we don't have a choice, we got to do it." Billy pulled himself up to a standing position then turned a meaningful look at his friend. "Well?" he asked.

"Oh, all right," Tom grumbled as he rose from the bench. "Let's get this over with."

Tom stepped off the wooden sidewalk with Billy following close behind. With Tom taking the lead, the two old men crossed the street and headed toward Sam's office.

"Good afternoon, gentlemen," Betty beamed at them from behind her desk. "And how are you two doing today?"

"Been better," Tom mumbled.

"Just fine," Billy replied with a friendly smile. "Sam in?"

"Why, yes he is. Just got back from a meeting not two minutes ago. Closed his door when he came in, for some reason. I expect he may be on the phone."

"Think you could check?" Billy asked pleasantly. "We need to talk with him if we could."

"Why, sure. Let me just see what he's up to." She rose from her chair and stepped around her desk. Stepping over to the closed door, she rapped lightly three times before opening it a few inches and peering inside.

"Tom and Uncle Billy would like to speak with you if you aren't tied up?" she said with a question in her voice.

"What do they want?" The irritated tone in Sam's voice was unmistakable.

"They didn't say," she replied as she leaned further into the room and lowered her voice. "They look like a couple of kids who have been caught with their hands in the cookie jar," she whispered. "I think they really need to talk to you, Sam."

"Oh, all right, send them in." Sam let out a long

sigh. All he wanted was to be left alone to lick his wounds. The absolute last thing he needed right now was having to put up with those two old trouble makers.

"Go on in." Betty gestured to the open door. "But don't keep him long, okay? He's got a ton of work to get caught up on," she added, hoping to shorten their visit as much as possible.

"What do you two want now," Sam growled, "my future first born? Not that there's likely to ever be one." His last words betrayed his emotions.

Before them sat a very dejected man, all right, one that needed as much help as they could offer.

"We just came by to see if there was anything we could do to help," Uncle Billy offered.

"Help?" Sam's voice raised a couple of decibels. "Are you kidding?"

"Now Sam…"

"Please! No more help! I stand to lose everything I've worked for here in Gold Bluff, but I can live with that. What I can't live with is the fact that by going along with your tall tales I've also lost the only woman I've ever loved."

"You can't mean Eden."

Sam slumped back into his chair. His chin lowered until it rested on his chest, he reached out to idly play with an assortment of paper clips that lay strewn across his desk.

"Of course I mean Eden, Tom. Who else could I mean?"

"But…well…I never…"

"No, Tom, you 'never.' You never thought before you spoke. You never considered what might happen when you spilled your guts to her, did you? It just never entered your mind that by making your grand confession you might be destroying the one chance I had at the good old American dream. You know the dream I'm talking about, Tom, the dream about 'happy ever after,' about a wife and kids and picket fences. That dream, Tom."

"Ah, Sammy, I'm so sorry. I never…what I mean is…"

"What he means is he never would have said a thing if he'd thought it would mess with you and Eden."

"I really wouldn't have, Sam. Why, I think the world of both you and Eden. It just never entered my mind that what I told her would affect the way you two felt about each other."

Sam sat there for a few moments, not speaking, just staring at the erratic arrangement of paper clips before him. A rueful smile tugged at his lips, but there was no humor reflected in his eyes.

"I just didn't expect to fall in love with the lady," he said with a sad sigh.

"I'll fix it, Sam," Tom promised. "I…"

"No, Tom, you won't fix it. Nobody can. Eden's let me know in no uncertain words what she thinks of the Gold Bluff deception, as she calls it, and everyone involved in it… most especially me. No, as far as Eden is concerned, there will be no 'fixing'."

"But…"

"No buts, Billy. You two have done enough. Let's just leave things the way they are, okay? I don't think I can survive any more of your help."

Sam slid further down in his chair as the two old men shut the door quietly behind themselves as they left his office. If anything, meeting with them had made him feel worse than before. Damn it, he loved those old guys. Why in hell did they have to go and screw everything up so bad? Why couldn't they have just left things alone?

And why did he have to feel like such a heel about coming down on them like that?

Because it was their fault, damn it! Well, not both of them actually, since it was Tom who had done the talking. But they were a team. What one thought the other acted upon, or so it always seemed. They were both guilty as sin.

Unfortunately, his conscience wouldn't let him get away with that reasoning. Nor with placing the full blame for his losing Eden on either of them. He'd known all along it was wrong to sell property based on a lie. He'd gone along with it. He was just as guilty as any of the others, which meant that Eden was completely accurate about him being unworthy of her love.

His last conversation with Eden ran relentlessly through his mind, not letting him forget one painful word. He had no excuse for what he'd done, so he hadn't even tried to give any. She was right; he was unprincipled and greedy. He couldn't blame her when she'd said she could never love a man so lacking in scruples.

Funny, he'd never thought of himself like that—a man without integrity. But that's who he was. How had he ever considered himself worthy of someone like Eden?

And now he'd gone and made those two old men feel responsible for his own misery. It wasn't either one of their faults, damn it. He was the one who had lied to Eden, not them. Well, maybe they'd fibbed a little, but that didn't really matter, did it? He was the one who was in love with her. He was the one who should have been honest with her from the very beginning. By maintaining his silence he had sabotaged any chance they'd ever had for a happy-ever-after.

Chapter Twelve

"So what do we do now?" Billy asked as he tried to match his shorter stride to Tom's longer one.

"We're going to talk to Eden, of course."

"I was afraid that's what you were going to say."

"You have a problem with that?"

"Maybe. After all, Sam did tell us to butt out, didn't he? Or did you hear something I missed?"

"I heard the same damn thing you did. That is, of course, if you have a fresh battery in your hearing aid."

"Then what makes you think it's such a good idea for us to go talk to Eden?"

Tom stopped walking so abruptly Billy barely avoided running right into him.

"It may not be a good idea at all. All I know is that, well, darn it anyway, I love that guy—always have ever since he was a little kid. If he loves that girl…darn it anyway, I got to do something to fix what he thinks we broke!"

Billy glanced up at Tom, taking stock of his friend's grim expression. After looking at him for a moment he nodded. "What the heck are you waiting for, old man?" He threw the words over his shoulder as he turned to walk briskly toward Eden's house.

*****

Eden lay sprawled face down on her bed, her face cradled on crossed arms. Tears from a completely justified good old fashioned crying session still stained her cheeks. The crying had worn her out but had done little to dispel her grief. Oh, she knew "time would heal all wounds" and all that crap, but right now she didn't believe there was enough time in the universe to heal the pain that tore at her heart.

Eden McKenna was not a woman who gave her heart freely. In all of her thirty-two years she had been in love just once before. That had been when she was just twelve years old and the object of her affections had been her next door neighbor, an eighteen-year-old Adonis. To her credit, Eden had not fallen for Kenny's good looks. What had gotten to her was the way he treated her. To her he'd seemed a grown man, yet still young enough to be interested in her as a person, not as a child.

When he talked to her, he always gazed directly into her eyes, as if he really cared about her. And he listened to her! He took time with her, telling her jokes, sharing her confidences. When he joined the Navy, it nearly broke her heart, but, just as he promised, he wrote her every week. At least he had for the first couple of months. Then the letters came less frequently, first monthly, and then less and less frequently. Finally, after Kenny had been gone for a little over a year, a letter came telling her he'd met a girl and he was going to ask her to marry him. He asked Eden to keep her fingers crossed she'd say yes. Eden never wrote back.

She didn't need to have her heart broken again to realize that giving your heart to a man was stupid—and it hurt. She would never do it again, and she hadn't.; at least not until now. And, damn, it still hurt.

When she heard the rapping on her front door, she ignored it. The only person she could think would be on her door step was Sam and she was not about to let him see her like this. Not that it would do him any good anyway. He was out of her life, and that was it!

The rapping was louder now and very persistent. She rose from the bed filled with righteous anger. He might think he'd come to talk to her, but she had other plans. It was her time to talk and he was going to get an ear full! She yanked the front door open, prepared to do battle royal.

"Who do you think you are to…? Oh, um…"

"Good evening, Eden," both old men said at once.

She could think of absolutely nothing to say. What could they possibly want? She just stood there staring at the two men.

"Could we come in, Eden honey?" Tom finally broke the silence.

"I...that is...actually, this isn't a good time."

"We know, honey. That's why we came."

"But..."

"Please? Won't you just give us a few minutes? It's really important."

Eden looked from Tom to Billy, who had remained silent, leaving Tom to do all the talking.

"It really is important, Eden. We wouldn't be bothering you if it wasn't," Billy urged.

"Come on in." She opened the door wider to allow the two men to pass through. She swiped at the moisture on her cheeks then reached up to push her tangled hair from her face. Darn, she hated for anyone to see her like this.

"Can I fix you some tea?"

"No, not today." Tom's voice sounded different, sort of strained.

Forcing her mind away from her own troubles, she gave each man a deeper scrutiny. Something was bothering both of them and it looked pretty serious. Had Sam told them she knew the truth about Gold Bluff? Were they afraid she'd go public with her information?

"You didn't come here to feed me more lies about Gold Bluff did you? Because if you did you might as well leave right now."

"No lies today, Eden, just the truth."

"Tom, how do you expect me to believe anything you say after all the stories you've told me? Heck, just about everyone in this town is so full of lies I don't think there's one of you who would know the truth if it stared you right in the face."

"I know it looks bad, Eden, but Tom here, he really does know what he's talking about. You really need to listen to him before you go off and do something you'll be sorry about for the rest of your life."

"Like letting the cat out of the bag about Gold Bluff's colorful history? Afraid I might mess up your precious financial investments?"

"Heck, I don't care about the money. I care about you and Sammy."

"Sammy? You've got to be kidding. There's not one thing you can tell me about Sam Gorton that's going to change my mind. So you might as well save yourself the trouble."

"Just give him five minutes, Eden. Please? Believe me, you'll be glad you did."

Eden gazed into Billy's watery blue eyes. She saw sincerity there, and a deep caring. As she recalled, Tom had always been the one with the wild stories, not Billy. Maybe she ought to listen to him.

"Five minutes, and that's all."

She could see relief flood Billy's eyes, but the expression in Tom's became even more serious.

"It's all my fault," Tom confessed, lowering his gaze to the floor before him.

Eden sighed, realizing that the five minutes Billy had pleaded for was an illusion. If she knew Tom Wenton, they were going to be here for quite some time.

"Please, sit down, both of you," she gestured to the two comfortable chairs that faced her sofa. She sat in the middle of the sofa so she could look directly into the eyes of both men while Tom made his "confession."

There the three of them sat, Eden looking from one man to the other, Tom looking everywhere but at Eden, Billy looking first at Tom, then Eden, then Tom, then Eden. Silence filled the room, broken only by the ticking of Eden's mantel clock.

"For pity's sake, say something!" Billy finally burst out in frustration. "It was your idea to come here, so get on with it!"

"Tom?" Eden prompted.

The old man shifted in his chair as if he were about to leave, then thought better of it and settled back down.

"I came here to tell you that you're all wrong about Sammy, Eden. He's a good boy. Heck, I almost feel like he's my very own son."

"But he lied to me. Actually, you lied to me too, so I don't see why I should place much credence on your recommendation."

"Well, now there's where you're wrong. Actually, he just *thought* he was lying to you when all the time he was telling you the truth."

"You're not making sense, Tom. Does any of this make sense to you, Uncle Billy?"

"Sorry to say, it does."

"What you got to understand is that I was the one that's been playing with the truth all along. I let everyone think the truth was a lie, so the lie is that the truth…well you understand, don't you?"

She shut her eyes for a moment, shook her head then opened them again. "No," she answered.

"Of course she doesn't understand, you old fool. Heck, I know what you're talking about and *I* don't understand. Do you think you could make it just a little more complicated?"

Tom drew in a deep breath then let it out slowly.

"Billy and I, we been knowing Sam and Joe ever since they were both a couple of kids."

"Sam was always my favorite of the two," said Billy.

"There wasn't anything wrong with Joe, Billy. You always did have to go and show favorites."

"So you guys have all known each other forever," Eden prompted Tom back to his tale. "Is that all you wanted to say? If it is…"

"No, I was just trying to let you know how things

got started around here, that's all. But all that does have a lot to do with what happened here in Gold Bluff."

"Tom, can't you just spit it out and get done with it? Do you have to turn it into a dang blamed saga?"

"This isn't easy! Will you please let me do it my way?"

Billy's shrug was all the answer Tom got.

"Okay, so what I was trying to say before someone so rudely interrupted me," Tom turned a baleful glare on Billy, before continuing, "was that we've been knowing those two boys since way back when. And when, years later, the two of them showed up here, all grown up and doing well for themselves, well we were just as pleased as could be.

"Billy and me, we had so much fun seeing them again, and visiting with Joe's family, that when it was time for them to leave I would've done just about anything to get them to stay. And from the way they were all acting, I figured the feeling was pretty much mutual. All they could talk about was how much they hated going back to the city and how much they wished they could just stay right here.

"I figured that maybe that wasn't such a bad idea. What I was thinking was, here I was an old man with a wife, my friend Billy, and a whole lot of land that was just sitting here not being used.

"I used to like it like that, just the three of us and all that land, but things change. We all kind'a liked having those kids around. So I made them a deal. I'd furnish the land if they'd do the developing. Together we figured we could make this place something special."

"Tom, this is all very interesting, but it doesn't change the fact that Sam lied to me about the history of Gold Bluff, or that all of the partners lied to the people who bought property here."

"Now you really shouldn't blame Sam for that," Billy interjected. "When all that stuff got printed in that magazine, Sam was the only one who wanted to go to them and get them to set the record straight."

"But how can I forgive him for letting me believe all those lies?"

"He only did it so the other guys would let him hire you. They wanted him to send you on your way and hire someone else, but he wouldn't do it. He said the kids deserved the best teacher they could get and you were it. So, to keep the other guys quiet, he agreed to do whatever he could to keep you from finding out the truth if they'd let him hire you."

"The history, well, it was all supposed to be a joke," Tom took over. "But the real joke is that there never really was a joke!"

Eden closed her eyes and began rubbing at her temples.

"Can't you just tell her the story straight?" Billy asked, his exasperation more than evident.

"Stop," Eden raised her hand. "Tom, I like you. Really, I do! But if I've learned nothing else from all of this, I've learned that I can't believe a word you say."

Tom sat up straight in his chair, a look of dismay filling his expressive eyes.

"I'm sorry, Tom, but it's true. You love to tell stories. You can't help it. It's just something you do."

"You got a bible somewhere in all those books?"

Billy suddenly stood up and began peering at the rows upon rows of books that threatened to overflow Eden's ample book cases.

"Of course I do," she said, opening a drawer in the table at the end of the sofa and pulling out a large, much used family bible.

"Here," he reached out and took the book from her hand and held it out before Tom, "swear on it that you're going to tell her the truth."

Without hesitation, Tom laid his left hand on the

bible. Raising his right hand he swore an oath of honesty. Both men turned to Eden with expressions that asked if they had proved their point.

"I don't know…" The doubt in her voice told them they had to go a step further.

"Here, let me do it," Billy said, handing the bible to Tom. Placing his left hand on the bible he lifted his right hand to his heart. "I swear that I know the whole story that Tom's going to tell you and I won't let him tell you one lie … or exaggeration neither," he added with a baleful gaze at his friend.

"Sometimes a good story just gets the better of him," he turned to Eden apologetically. "Only I won't let it happen this time. You can depend on me on this," he promised.

Eden looked from one old man to the other, a smile beginning to tug at the corners of her mouth. What a pair!

"Oh, all right, I'll listen to your story, Tom. But don't you dare forget your oath!"

Chapter Thirteen

"It all started when my grandparents, Abigail and Jedidiah Wenton decided to leave the petered out gold fields in the Sierras and head up to Oregon."

"For Pete's sake, she wanted to know the truth, not the history of the Wenton family back to the beginning of time."

"If I'm going to tell the story I'll tell it my way, if you don't mind."

"But she's heard all that before."

"She did, but since she thinks we've all lied to her, she needs to hear the real story, right from the start, just like it happened. Now that we've both given our oaths, she'll know what I'm saying is the truth. You can't blame her for doubting what I said before I took that oath, now can you?"

"You're just wasting her…"

"I've got an idea that might move things along," Eden interjected. "I've heard the story about how your family first came here. Can I assume that what you told the kids in my classroom is the truth? Because, if it is, then why don't we skip that part and get on with the part that concerns the townspeople right now."

Tom, being the type of man who enjoyed nothing better than having a captive audience was a little perturbed about not being allowed to tell the entire story, from the day of his very first ancestor's birth (which would have been sometime during the time before the wheel was invented), up until the very moment of the telling. However, Billy's stern expression told him that now was not the time for him to indulge himself.

"Alright, if that's the way you want it, I guess I can cut through the first part and skip on to the part of the story that matters the most—the part about how Gold Bluff actually came to be.

"So, a couple of years after my Grandpappy died, and the local Indians saw how poorly Grandma and he kids were doing, the leader of the village took her to the bluffs and showed her something that changed her life forever—a vein of almost pure gold. After that she and the kids worked the mine, taking only enough to keep them living comfortably. She'd been around the great strike of '49, so she knew what would happen if word got out about her find. Of course, a person can be only so careful, and eventually word did leak out and a mad rush of prospectors descended on Gold Bluff. The town grew up behind the mining like a bunch of mushrooms.

"And, pretty much, that's the true history of Gold Bluff, California." Tom leaned back in his chair, apparently satisfied with his rendition of the tale.

"But you've left out why the houses are all in the wrong places!"

"Oh, that's simple. They're that way because…well…"

"It's because he screwed up, that's why," Billy interjected.

"I did not!"

"Sure you did. If you'd been thinking right, you would have made sure Sam and the partners put the houses where they'd been in the first place!"

"If you'll remember, I told you about the fire when we were going through Aunt Ruth's things. The whole place burned down. Everything, that is, except my Aunt Ruth's house."

"The Stossard mansion."

"Right, it being made of stone and all, it stood while the rest of the place burned up like so much dry tinder."

"But what…?"

"Eden, honey, I think this old man has talked about as much as he can in one sitting," Tom said as he slowly rose to his feet. "If you don't mind, I think I'd better get on home. Ella'll probably have my hide for being out so late as it is."

Eden still had questions, but didn't have the heart to keep the two old men any longer.

"Thank you, Tom." She pulled him into an embrace then turned to do the same with Billy. "You're both a couple of sweethearts for coming here like this."

"We just wanted to help," Tom said, his voice more gruff than usual.

"We didn't want to see you two kids get off on the wrong foot," Billy added. "We'd hate to see the two of you split up over a little misunderstanding."

Eden watched them as they walked away from her house. They were a pair, all right. She couldn't help but love them both, but could she believe a word they said? And anyway, even if everything Tom had told her was true, what difference did it make? Sam had still lied to her, by omission if not by commission. He'd not only let her believe in the authenticity of the buildings, there was no way to know how he and his partners had profited from of their scheme. And in her world, that was something that could simply not be forgiven.

******

"You had to go and do it again, didn't you?" Uncle Billy grumbled as they walked away from Eden's house. "I thought that just once in your life you were going to do the right thing."

"What are you talking about? I told her the truth, just like I said I would."

"But not the *whole* truth! You left out one of the most important parts. You never even mentioned your Aunt Ruth's secret. You swore on the bible you'd tell the truth, the whole truth, and part of that truth is the secret."

"Now wait just a minute there! I swore to the truth, not the whole truth."

"There you go again, quibbling. You swore on the

bible to tell the truth. When you do that, everyone just naturally expects that to include the 'whole' truth right along with it."

"Then they'd be fools."

"Are you calling me a fool?" Billy's voice raised a couple of notches.

Tom's reply was a hearty "Humph!"

They continued walking in silence until Uncle Billy simply could not stand it another moment.

"Why? That's all I want to know. Why didn't you tell her the whole story?"

"I'm not ready yet."

"Ready! My God, man, you're ninety-two years old. At the rate you're going you'll be dead before you're ready!

Chapter Fourteen

Eden didn't sleep much that night. Actually, she barely slept at all. She'd never been so confused. Sam had lied to her and she couldn't tolerate a liar. But one could argue he hadn't really lied. He'd let her believe a lie…that wasn't really a lie at all. Or was it? And so her night had gone, her thoughts twisting and turning, hour after hour.

She climbed out of bed at the first hint of morning. A full pot of strong coffee did little to dispel the cobwebs that had taken root in her brain during the long hours of the night. A hot shower didn't do much more to help.

She dreaded going to school that day, which broke her heart. She'd loved her job, loved getting up early and going over her lesson plans, looking forward to challenging her students to do their best work. She didn't feel much like challenging them this morning. How could she after all their hard work had turned up nothing but lies and deception? What a mess.

"Are you going to the meeting tonight," one of her students asked as they walked up the schools broad steps together.

"What meeting is that?" she asked.

"Haven't you seen any of the fliers? They're all over town. They say there's a Town Hall meeting tonight here in the auditorium. They say it's about something of importance to the entire population of Gold Bluff. You don't think it could be about the messed up houses, do you? You know, that stuff we figured out yesterday?"

Eden's pulse stepped up a notch. What else could it be?

*****

Sam sat in the straight backed chair at the right hand side of the high school auditorium's stage, watching people filtering down the aisles and finding seats for themselves. They spoke to one another in hushed tones as they glanced with open curiosity to the men who shared the stage with Sam. His stomach clenched when he thought of the words he would soon be saying up there at the podium. Damn! He'd rather be about anywhere else than here in Gold Bluff right now.

His emotions warred with themselves. How were these people going to take what he was about to tell them? Would they think it was all a great gag? Or would they want to hang every man who sat up here with him? If they all wanted their money back, so be it. He'd pay back every last one of them if he had to hock everything he had and ever would have, if that's what they wanted.

The money wasn't what mattered any more. What mattered to him now was what these people thought of him. Over these last three years, they had become like family. The thought of their thinking of him as nothing more than some cheap hustler caused him physical pain.

And then there was Eden. Words couldn't begin to describe the emptiness he felt every time he thought of losing her. What a fool he'd been to let his greed come between him and the only woman he'd ever loved. Time after time, he'd let the other partners stop him from doing what he knew in his heart he should. He cursed himself for being a liar and a coward.

His chest tightened when she entered the room surrounded by several of her students. Her face was closed, her body held together tightly, and she looked everywhere but him.

He wished she'd look up at him, if only for a moment. He longed to look into her eyes just once more, to watch the shadows play in their depths as he spoke to her, telling her how very much he loved her and how deeply sorry he was he had failed her. But the closed expression he saw on her face told him that would never happen.

He watched as she led her students down the aisle to the very first row of seats. His heart swelled with pride at her bravery. His and Eden's interest in one another had not been a secret in Gold Bluff. He could only imagine how embarrassing all of this must be to her. But there she was, sitting with her head held high and her spine ramrod straight, right down in front where everyone could see her. God, how he admired her courage.

He felt his heart swell with admiration, then suddenly wither and die. He'd lost her—the only woman who had ever touched his heart. He'd had his chance at the best life could offer and he'd thrown it away.

Well, hell.

He rose from his chair and approached the podium. It had already been agreed between the partners that although they would all share the stage with him, he would be the one to lead the meeting. The rest of them would be there to answer any questions directed to them personally, but as far as they were concerned this was his show.

"Good evening, ladies and gentlemen…neighbors and friends," he began. His heart was racing; his pulse beat a crazy rhythm in his ears. This was going to be harder than he'd thought.

"I know this meeting has come as a surprise, and I apologize for that. I wish we'd been able to give you more notice, but the truth of it is there are some things that have recently come out and we, my partners and I, we figured we needed to get the whole town together and put our cards on the table before the rumor mill got hold of them."

"What's this all about, Sam?"

"Get to the point!"

Smiling, Sam raised his hands to quiet the crowd. "I'm trying to, Anthony, if you'll just give me a minute."

"This meeting will most directly affect those of you who bought buildings in this town that were part of the original town of Gold Bluff. The rest of you, the ones who bought the newer places, might have an interest in what I'm about to tell you too."

There was a stirring in the crowd as people turned concerned glances to one another.

"There's nothing shaky about the titles to our properties, is there?" Miriam Wilson called out.

"No, no, not at all. Everyone who bought property in Gold Bluff has a totally unencumbered title to their property."

"Then what is it, dammit?" Anthony interrupted once again.

"It's about Gold Bluff's history," Sam blurted out. This was not how he'd planned on doing this, but what the hell?

A low murmur spread through the audience as people turned to one another with confused expressions on their faces.

"History?"

"What the hell's he talking about?"

"You mean I'm missing my favorite TV show for some stupid history lesson?"

"This is more than a history lesson, folks," Sam continued. "This is more in the line of a confession."

Suddenly the room was as quiet as a church on a Monday morning. Eden's complete attention was riveted on Sam. She heard no other sound than his words. The hundred or more people who surrounded her faded from her awareness. It was as if he was speaking to her and to her alone. Yet she knew that wasn't so. She knew that by standing up there confessing his part in the deception to the people who shared this room with her he stood to lose everything he'd worked so hard to achieve. And yet he was doing it. She was so proud of him she could burst.

She listened to his words, memorizing each and every one. He left nothing out, starting from the very beginning of the partners' concept of Golf Bluff up to this very moment. He could have sugar coated it, but he didn't.

"Now, I guess that just about sums it up," he

concluded. "There's just one more thing I'd like to say. If there's anyone here who feels I've cheated them and they want out of here, I promise to personally refund every last dime they gave us. I love this town just the way it is, history or no history, and I don't want anyone to feel that they're stuck here. So, please come see me if Gold Bluff is not where you want to be."

He started to move away from the podium, then stepped back to it to say, "I think you've heard enough from me, so I'm going to let the other guys answer your questions now, but I'll be waiting in the lobby if there's anyone who wants to see me after the meeting. After you've asked all the questions you want, we'll give the auditorium to you so you can discuss all this amongst yourselves. We're not here tonight to try to talk any of you into doing anything you don't want to do. Personally, I wish every one of you would stay right here in Gold Bluff. You're my neighbors and my friends and I don't want to lose any one of you. But staying is your decision and your decision alone.

"Thanks for hearing me out," he said as he backed away from the podium.

After Sam stepped down from the stage and walked to the door at the back of the room Joe took his place at the podium.

"Sam said it all, folks. The rest of us guys up here on the stage will be happy to take any questions you might have." He looked over the audience, searching for raised hands.

*****

Well, that was it, Sam thought as he passed his neighbors and friends on his way out of the auditorium. Before he went home tonight he might be flat broke—and then some. He should be worried sick, but for some crazy reason he wasn't. Actually, he felt pretty darned good. He'd never wanted to perpetuate that crazy story. Now that it was out he felt clean, as if he'd taken a long, cleansing shower. His only regret was the loss of Eden's respect—and love. That was one thing he would never stop regretting.

One by one, the other partners joined him. The relaxed camaraderie they usually shared was totally absent as they stood together. A wry smile touched Sam's lips as he looked from one man to another, noting the somber expressions on each of their faces. So this was what their foolishness had come to, five scared guys standing out here in the high school's auditorium waiting to find out if they still had futures in this town.

The door opened once again, and Tom Wenton and Bill Johnson joined the waiting men. Tom raised his eyes to the other men with a sheepish expression then lowered his gaze to the carpeted floor. The sounds of multiple voices talking at once rose as the door opened, then settled into a low mumble as the door swung closed again.

"We may be in for a long wait," was Bill's only comment as the door closed off the noise from the room he had just left.

Eden listened as first one person and then another voiced their opinions of what they had just been told. As she listened to the angry voices, one shouting over another until it became nearly impossible to make sense of anything, she began to lose her patience. Although a few of the people made intelligent comments, many of the others were simply absurd.

"They just want to get their hands on our property," Anthony Thomas shouted. Just you watch. They're going to low ball every one of us!"

"Yeah, that's what it is, a scam to run us out of here," someone yelled from the back of the crowd.

"We ought to run their butts out of town, that's what we ought to do!"

Eden couldn't listen to anymore. She hated to

become any more embroiled in this mess, but still, she couldn't just sit there and watch anarchy take over. Rising slowly to her feet, she reluctantly walked up the steps to the stage and approached the abandoned microphone.

""Please, may I say something?" she said quietly into the microphone.

A chorus of shushes and "Let's hear what Ms. Eden has to say" quickly quieted the room.

She stood before them wondering if she even had the right to speak. Not being a property owner she had no financial involvement in the affair. Her only claim to the town was that she was a teacher there, and a new one at that. All she really had to offer was her knowledge and her passion. She hoped either or both would be of some use.

"For those of you who don't know me, my name is Eden McKenna, and I'm the high school English and history teacher here in Gold Bluff. Although I'm not myself a property owner, I feel since it was my students' special project that brought all this to light I must claim some responsibility for whatever happens here tonight.

"For most of my life my books were the most important things to me. When other children were out playing with their toys, you could usually find me in some corner with a book in front of my nose. And always, my favorite books were those that told the stories of the past. As I grew up history became my passion, often excluding friends or any other outside activity.

"So, as you can imagine nothing can be more important to me than the accuracy of history. At least that's what I thought. Now I'm not so sure.

"Just to help get a little perspective about what Sam and the others have told us tonight, I'd like to ask you all a couple of questions. First of all, by a show of hands, I'd like to see how many people here bought their homes or businesses purely because of the town's history."

She waited a few moments for the hands to rise.

Letting her eyes scan the entire room, she noted that less than half a dozen raised were hands.

"Good," she said with a smile. "Although there aren't that many who actually bought into Gold Bluff because of what they'd been told about the history, I'm happy to tell you, you made a good decision. To the very best of my knowledge, the history you were told is accurate.

"Now, also by a show of hands, I'd like to see who invested in property solely because they believed their purchase was an actual historical treasure."

Once again she scanned the room, noting two raised hands—one of them being Anthony Thomas, which did not come as a surprise. The other hand belonged to John Pettegrew, the town pharmacist. Eden cringed a bit at the sight of John's raised hand. Mr. Pettegrew and his family were great assets to Gold Bluff. She'd really hate to see them leave, taking the only pharmacy with them.

"Okay, you can put your hands down now. All I can say to you, Mr. Thomas and Mr. Pettegrew, is that if you bought your property on that assumption, then you might want to think about taking Sam up on his offer. All of the buildings we believed to be nineteenth century structures, with the exception of the Stossard mansion, are nothing more than replicas.

"However, there is a bright side to that. Because they're new structures, they are far sturdier than older buildings would be."

"You got that right," Erick Hampton, Todd's father, spoke up. "I wondered why I got by with such a low heating bill last winter."

"They're a lot safer, too," Emily Wilson called out. "I bet those old buildings never had to meet the safety standards our new houses did."

"You see?" Eden asked. "There can be benefits to owning newer homes over vintage ones.

"Now, I have one more question. How many of you decided to move to Gold Bluff because of what the town offered, forgetting the history entirely?"

To Eden's relief, the room was suddenly filled with raised hands. It was just as she'd hoped.

"Now, I suppose what you have to ask yourselves is, what's really important to you, the lifestyle Gold Bluff has to offer or the knowledge that your home is less historically accurate than you had believed. Personally, given that choice, I know what my own answer would be. But it's not my place to tell any one of you what to do. It's your town, and your decision.

"Thank you for listening to me," she said with a smile before stepping away from the podium. She glanced at her students as she passed them by, giving them a quick, almost apologetic smile. She hoped they didn't think she'd sold them out, but she had to say what she felt needed to be said, even though it might not have been what they had expected.

She'd been the one preaching about the importance of researching accuracy, and she still believed in it. But if being completely accurate about Gold Bluff's so called "historical" character meant the destruction of such a wonderful town, then it simply wasn't worth the price. People were what mattered, and Gold Bluff was filled with some of the most wonderful people she'd ever met.

As she passed through the auditorium door she was faced with the full lineup of Gold Bluff partners, but there was only one face that mattered to her. Without bothering to acknowledge any of the others, she stepped up to Sam.

She looked up at his handsome face. It hurt her heart to see the pain in his eyes, knowing she had been partly the cause of it. She'd misjudged him so terribly. Oh, she knew he wasn't perfect, but then, who was? But when it came down to the bottom line, Sam had come through with shining colors. He'd stood up there and faced his neighbors, not trying to excuse himself but rather trying to right the wrong he'd done.

"I think I owe you an apology," was all she could think to say. She wanted to say more, but was interrupted by a sudden tidal wave of people as they came pouring through the doors of the auditorium. Before she knew what was happening, they were surrounded by dozens of people.

"You can't get rid of us," one man said with a smile and a handshake.

"What's the big deal about a bunch of run down old buildings, anyway?" another laughed as he slapped Sam and Joe Stanton on their backs.

"I want my money back," Anthony Thomas called out belligerently from the outside edge of the assembly. "You can fool all of them, but you can't fool me."

"See me in my office tomorrow morning, Anthony. I'll have a check ready for you."

"Yeah, well, you better double what I paid for my house or we're going to court!"

"Tomorrow, Anthony—ten o'clock," Sam replied good-naturedly. Grinning down at Eden he said, "Heck, I'd triple the price just to get that guy out of town. He's been nothing but a pain from the get-go."

Eden watched John Pettegrew work his way toward Sam and herself. She felt a tightening in her stomach. Was he going to leave too? John reached his hand out to Sam. "Old construction or new, I guess none of it matters as much as the people in this town. I can't even think of leaving all the friends the family and I have made since moving here. Yep, it looks as if the Pettegrew bunch is here for the duration."

"You can't know how relieved I am to hear that, John. You and your family are real assets to Gold Bluff. I don't even want to think about losing any one of you."

Greeting his friends and neighbors, taking a jibe here and there, laughing at their jokes, Sam managed to make some sort of contact with each and every person there, yet still keep Eden at his side. "We need to talk," he spoke in her ear when she tried to step away from him, allowing more space for the others. "Don't go away, okay?"

Oh, she wasn't going anywhere. She would stay by his side for as long as it took. It took nearly forty-five minutes before the last of Gold Bluff's citizens finally went out into the night. With brief words, the partners also left until only Sam and Eden remained to make sure the doors were all properly locked. Sam closed the last door firmly, checking to make sure the lock held, then turned to walk down the broad steps at Eden's side. Together they walked silently into the night.

She wanted to reach out for his hand, but held back. What if what he wanted to talk to her about was to tell her he'd had enough of her meddling and didn't want anything more to do with her? She couldn't exactly blame him if that's how he felt. After all, everything had been going along fine in Gold Bluff until she'd come along.

She'd just about reached the conclusion that any hope there'd been for a relationship between them had been destroyed when she felt his hand take hold of hers. Her heart swelled with relief as she let her fingers tighten in his. The silence continued, but now it felt safer than it had before.

"Can I come in for a minute?" he asked when they reached her door.

"For as long as you like," she replied.

"Now don't go tempting me, Ms. McKenna. If I stayed as long as I like, your reputation would be completely destroyed. We don't want that, do we?"

"Don't we?" was all she said as she lifted her lips for his kiss the moment the front door closed behind them.

Chapter Fifteen

"I'm thinking it might be time to tell Eden the rest of the truth," Tom said to his wife, Ella, and Uncle Billy the next morning. The three old friends were sitting around the Wenton's breakfast table, nursing one more mug of coffee before getting on with that day's chores. Which, in the two men's cases meant their going into Gold Bluff and taking up their usual places on the bench in front of the Emporium.

"Are you sure that's for the best?" Ella asked. "I was certain you'd go to your grave before you'd tell Aunt Ruth's secret."

"What made you change your mind about telling her?" Billy questioned.

"I came close to telling her a couple of times, but I just couldn't do it. But after the way she stood up to all them folks at the meeting, well, I figure there ain't anyone more trustworthy than that girl—unless it was ol' Sammy."

"So you're going to tell her, but you're *not* going to tell him?" Billy glanced over at Ella with a puzzled shake of his head.

"I plan on telling 'em both!"

*****

"I can't believe I'm actually about to meet the legendary Ella Wenton," Eden said with an impish grin as she and Sam walked the short distance from his car to the Wenton cabin. "I was beginning to wonder if I'd ever meet the lady."

"You! I've known Tom almost all my life, and this is the very first time I've ever been invited to their home."

"You're kidding!"

"Nope, in fact, up until now I've never even known where this place was. Ever since we've been kids, Joe and I've speculated about it, but neither one of us was ever able to figure out where it was."

"Well, it's no wonder you couldn't find it. What with having to get past three locked gates and traveling along that horrible old lumber road just to get here, it's a small wonder Tom and Billy find their own way home."

"You got that right, especially after those old codgers have put away more than their share of beers. Now that I've driven down the road they have to take each time they come home, I'm thinking I'll never want to see either of them drinking anything stronger than a cup of coffee before heading home."

The front door to the two story log cabin opened inward as the two young people approached the house. A small woman stepped out on the porch, holding the screen door open as she gestured for her guests to enter.

Just barely five feet tall in her youth, Ella Wenton's body had settled down to a compact four feet, nine inches. Hair that showed signs of having once been blond but was now silvery white had been braided into one long plait and wound into a crown at the top of her head. Her face, completely devoid of makeup and lavishly etched with wrinkles, radiated its own beauty, a beauty which was enhanced by a warm smile and sparkling blue eyes "Come on in," the older woman called to them as they approached the house. "We're all sitting out on the screened porch, taking a little rest before I put out dinner. You two just come on in and let me get you a nice cold glass of iced tea."

They were both ushered in, handed frosted glasses of tea, and led out to the welcoming coolness of the shaded porch.

"Took you long enough to get here," Tom grumbled as he rose from his chair, a massive old overstuffed thing that had probably been sitting in the exact same spot for the last fifty years at least. The well-defined indentations in its cushions gave evidence that Tom's slender frame had made use of its comfort for many years. Sitting opposite Tom was Uncle Billy.

"Come on, you two, get yourselves comfortable." Billy indicated that they should both sit on a loveseat just to the right of Tom's chair, totally ignoring the much roomier sofa that sat on his left. The pleased expression Eden saw in Billy's eyes as they sat down together, so close their thighs could not help but nudge one another, was quite obvious.

"What are you two up to now?" Eden thought to herself as she settled into the loveseat.

"Oh, good, you're all nice and settled," Ella sang out as she returned to the room, sitting down on one end of the sofa. "Now, isn't this nice! I can't tell you how pleased I am that you've come out for a visit."

"You've really got a lovely place out here, Mrs. Wenton. But it's so far from everyone. Don't you ever get lonesome?"

"Me? Lonesome? Oh, my no. I have way too much to keep me busy to even think of getting lonesome."

"Set in her ways, is what she is," Tom interrupted.

"Now, Tom, it's not like that at all, and you know it. It's just that I have my gardens to tend and the chickens to care for. And then, there's the bees of course. "

"Not to mention every wild critter living within a radius of twenty miles," Billy offered.

"Them too," Ella cheerfully agreed. "I don't know what I'd do without all my babies."

"Humph! Babies! Before you leave you two need to let her introduce you to her latest 'baby.' She's got herself the biggest darned raccoon I've ever laid eyes on. The danged thing follows her around like a lovesick puppy."

"Don't you be making fun of Barnaby," Ella scolded her husband playfully. "He can't help it if he thinks I'm his momma."

She turned her attention back to her young guests. "His poor momma was shot by some fool, and the poor little thing was left to starve to death. Luckily, I found him before it was too late. So he just naturally thinks of me as his adoptive momma."

"The big baby," Tom grumbled.

"Okay, enough of this chit-chat," Billy interrupted. "Let's get on with what we were planning on discussing with these two."

Apparently Uncle Billy had heard enough about Barnaby and was ready to get on to the important stuff.

"Right," Ella nodded cheerfully. "Time's a wasting." She and Billy both shifted their attention to Tom.

Tom sat still for a moment as all eyes in the room rested on him. Usually he reveled in being the center of attention, always being quick to fill any silence with some comment or other.

"Okay," Tom finally broke the silence, "here goes." Once again he fell silent as he let his gaze settle first on Sam and then on Eden.

"Spit it out, will you?" Billy urged impatiently.

"I'm getting to it! I'm just trying to choose my words, that's all."

"Leave him be, Billy. You know this is hard for Tom. He'll get it out in his own good time."

"Thank you, mother," Tom smiled tenderly at Ella. "See why I keep her?" he turned back to Sam and Eden. "My bride here, she knows me better'n anyone else."

Eden couldn't help smiling at the old couple. How wonderful it must be to still love your partner after all the years the Wenton's had been together.

"All right, I'm ready," Tom said gruffly. "I guess it's time I told you two the rest of the Gold Bluff story."

"What?"

"Don't tell me you've been lying all along!"

"Now, now, hear him out," Ella urged. "It's not as bad you might be thinking."

By the stormy clouds Eden saw in Sam's eyes, she suspected he was thinking the word 'bad' might be way too tame to describe what was going through his mind."

"I never lied—not really, anyway. Everything I ever said about the Wenton family was true."

"And neither one of us ever lied to you about the first Gold Bluff," Billy interrupted. "The place really did exist, and there actually was a huge gold strike there in the bluffs."

"What we never told you was just how it was that Gold Bluff burned down. Or why we've kept it a secret."

"Don't you hate secrets?" Ella asked Eden. A concerned frown etched her brow. "They just seem to fester. Getting bigger and bigger until they just have to come out."

"But why…? I mean, what could have been so terrible that it had to be kept a secret? Is it something that could ruin today's Gold Bluff?" Eden's concern was genuine. She'd come to love this place and dreaded the thought that something ugly might spoil it.

"It wasn't my secret," Tom continued. "If it had'a been, I'd a told you long ago. No, it was a secret I was bound to long ago by my Aunt Ruth. Just before she died she told me the story I'm about to tell you now. When she was through telling me, I realized how important it was to everyone that I honor her wishes."

"Why, we were married for ten years before Tom ever told me!" Ella stated proudly. "And the only reason he told me then was because I was talking about us moving away from here. I really had it in my head that I wanted to see a whole lot more of the world than I'd be seeing if we stayed here. That was when Tom told me…, well, what he's about to tell you now."

"He told me when you and your partners started talking about developing the town," Uncle Billy added. "He really liked the idea of building the town back to what it had once been, but was worried the secret might get out and ruin everything—just like it did the first time."

Now they really had Sam's and Eden's attention. What in the world could these three be talking about?

"It's about the gold mine," Tom tried to continue.

"But we already know about the gold mind," Sam interrupted. "Don't tell me there was something fishy about that."

"No, everything I told you about that was true. Everything, that is, except that there were actually two strikes, not just one."

"Two?"

"Two!"

"That's right, two. The first one was the one you already heard about. That was the one that put the town on the map. And, just like I already told you, that's the one that finally petered out."

"And when it went, so did most of the town's population." Billy interjected.

"Until there were only three people left living here, my Aunt Ruth, her husband, Bull Stossard and his best friend and partner, Ewell Parsons."

"Kind'a reminds you of the three of us, don't it?" Ella piped in. "Lucky for Billy here, though, Tom and that old bully, Bull Stossard, were cut from a different cloth."

"About a year after everyone else cut out, Uncle Bull was doing a little prospecting, more to keep himself busy than from any real expectations, and he came across a strike that made the first one look puny."

"But I don't understand. If he made another strike, why hasn't anyone ever heard about it?" Sam asked.

"You see, my Uncle Bull wasn't called 'bull' for nothing. He had a mind that would make an ornery bull look plumb pliable. He found that gold on land he'd laid claim to years before and he wasn't about to share one ounce of it with anyone—not even his old partner.

"When Ewell found out about it, it didn't hit him right. He figured that partners shared, no matter who found the gold or where they found it. As far as he was concerned, he'd stuck it out with Bull so it was only fair that Bull should share the gold with him.

"Well, they got into a knock down, drug out fight, right there in the middle of Main Street. Aunt Ruth, she heard the ruckus and she came running. She cried when she told me about it all those years later. She told me how she tried to make them stop, but neither one of them would listen to her. They just kept swinging on one another, landing a punch now and again, but for the most part not doing much damage.

"But then something awful happened. When it looked like Ewell wouldn't ever give up, Uncle Bull picked up a big stick that was laying there on the side of the road and hit Ewell smack dab between the eyes. It must'a been a real corker, 'cuz it knocked him out cold.

"At first Bull just stood there cussing at his old partner, telling him what a good for nothing friend he'd turned out to be. But Ewell, he wasn't hearing a word of what Bull was saying. No, sir, Ewell didn't hear nothing from that day forward, 'cuz he was dead as a man could be."

"Oh, my God!" Eden exclaimed.

"Right, it was a terrible thing. And it only got worse." Ella interjected.

"That it did," Tom continued. "Naturally my aunt was horrified. She was all ready to send for the sheriff up in Yreka, but Uncle Bull wasn't about to let her. He flat out refused to let her and she never forgave him for it. She knew it was the right thing to do, but she was too afraid of Bull to go against him.

"For Bull's part, killing his best friend was like killing himself. Up until then, he'd never been much of a drinking man, but after he buried Ewell he turned to alcohol with a vengeance. Aunt Ruth said hardly a day went by that Bull didn't drink himself into a stupor. Just about every day he'd get himself stinking drunk then wander the town, now all empty and all, talking out loud just like there were people there to listen to him.

"She got to where she couldn't stand the sight of him, so one night, after he'd been out cursing the empty town at the top of his lungs, she locked the door and wouldn't let him in. She yelled at him through the locked door that he could come back when he was sober and not a minute sooner.

"Then he did something she never thought him capable of. He took every bottle of hooch he could lay his hands on and used them to torch the whole town. When she saw the flames, Aunt Ruth ran out to find him, to keep him from burning himself up along with everything else.

"She told me she ran all over the town, avoiding flying embers as best as she could, calling his name, begging him to forgive her. When she finally found him, he was standing outside the burning schoolhouse. She said she'd never forget the look on his face when he saw her running down the street toward him. He just looked her dead in the eyes, then turned and walked back into the school, letting the flaming timbers crush him. When she knew there wasn't anything she could do to save him, she just sat down in the middle of the street and let the whole town burn down around her. The only building left standing was her own, the stone mansion he'd built her during their good days."

Silence filled the room as they all pondered the story they'd just heard. Although the three older people had heard it before, its effect was still very powerful. Tom finally broke the silence.

"And now you see why I couldn't tell anyone else the whole story. It was my Aunt Ruth's secret, one she would have died with except for the worry she had that the gold might one day be found again, and that more people would suffer. She truly believed the stuff was cursed, and it was her duty to prevent its ever being found again.

"You might say she passed the responsibility on to me before she died. That was why she left me all her holdings. She figured that if someone else ever got their hands on the land where Bull made his strike, the ugliness would start up all over again. Now it's my time to pass the secret—and the responsibility—on to someone else."

"But why are you telling us?" Eden asked. "Shouldn't you be telling your own heirs?"

"That's just the problem, dear," Ella answered. "Tom and I, we were never blessed with children. Neither one of us has anyone—at least no one we feel we can trust with such an important secret."

"That's why we've chosen you two."

"Now look," Sam protested, "you can't do this. Hell, Tom... Billy, both of you know I'm the last person on earth you should be leaving a gold mine to. You know I've pulled more than a couple of shady deals in my time. Since when did I become so darned trustworthy?"

"Since you tied up with Eden," Billy answered for both Tom and Ella.

"But you can't..."

"Yes we can," Tom replied emphatically.

"But I don't want a gold mine." Eden felt as if her name had been changed to Alice and she'd just fallen down a very strange rabbit's hole.

"Yes, we know!" Ella smiled her delight. "And that's exactly why we're giving it to you."

"To you and Sammy," Tom corrected.

Turning his gaze to Eden, Sam was confronted with the most exquisitely pleading expression he'd ever encountered. "You don't want a gold mine either, do you Sam?" she asked him.

"Not really," was his reply.

"You see? Neither one of us wants this gold mine of your uncle's, so you need to think of someone else to leave it to."

"You're both missing the point of all this." Tom was beginning to sound more than a little aggravated. "We're giving you the mine *because* you don't want one. If you wanted one, we wouldn't be giving it to you."

"We're giving it to you for safe keeping, dear. What we needed was to find someone who would keep it a secret, just as we have."

"But both of us? Together? What makes you think that's such a good idea? Wouldn't you be better off giving it to just one of us? Or, if you think two people would be better than just one, why not pick a nice married couple?"

"Except for the married part, you two *are* a nice couple." Ella beamed happily at the two of them. "That's why Tom picked you."

"When I heard you'd decided not to leave town that really made up my mind. Both you and Sam love this town, Eden, maybe even as much as I love it. Something in my gut tells me I can trust this with the two of you.

Sam and Eden looked into each other's eyes, communicating silently. After a moment Eden smiled. Sam nodded. "We'd be honored," Sam said, letting his gaze shift from first Tom, then to Ella, and finally to Billy.

"Let's take them out to see what all this fuss is about," Ella suggested. "We'll have to take your car, Sam. There's too many of us to fit in Tom's old buggy."

"You can actually reach it easier by going back through town, but I don't like going that way—too likely to draw attention to it. By taking the back route no one will see us, which is the way I like it."

The road was bumpy and all but non-existent in some places. In and around the mountains they drove until Eden lost all sense of direction. They skirted a swiftly running creek then turned from it and headed into deep forest. Huge trees towered over them, creating a narrow tunnel.

It seemed they'd been driving forever when the car finally emerged at a large meadow. Circled on three sides by the forest, the west edge of the property appeared to drop off abruptly. About fifty feet from the edge was a huge pile of boulders. Tough Manzanita bushes grew amongst the rocks, their roots holding onto every spare inch of earth.

"Keep your voices down and stay away from the edge over there," Tom instructed as they all climbed out of Sam's car. He reached for the short handled spade he'd brought from his home.

"We're at the top of the Bluffs," Tom replied to Eden's questioning glance. "If there was someone down there they might be able to hear our voices. And we sure as heck don't want them to see us up here. The one thing we don't want is a bunch of curious kids coming up to see what's goin' on."

"Come on," Ella called softly, gesturing that they should all follow her as she headed toward the mound of boulders.

Uncle Billy got there first and began pulling away a tangle of Manzanita bushes, casting them to one side. By the time the rest of them reached him he had managed to clear away enough of them to reveal a space between the rocks that appeared to have been filled with dirt.

"Here," Tom said as he handed the spade to Sam, "start digging."

Sam took the tool and began casting shovels full of dirt to one side. It took only a few minutes of work before the blade of the spade hit solid rock.

"Here, let me show you," Tom stepped up to the hole Sam had made and began brushing the remaining dirt from the cavity. "Come over here and take a look," he instructed both Eden and Sam as he stepped away from the cleaned out hole.

"Oh, my God," was all Sam could say as his mind

struggled to accept what he was seeing.

"Is that what I think it is?" Eden asked with awe in her voice.

"That's just the tip of the iceberg, honey...the *tip* of the iceberg.

Both Sam and Eden leaned in closer to get a better look. Glancing up for a moment, their eyes met, the expressions on both of their faces registering utter amazement. Then simultaneously, they both looked back down into the hole.

"Quite a sight, isn't it?" Billy queried in his dry manner. "Could change a person's outlook on life, if they let it."

"Huh?" Sam barely seemed aware of anything other than the amazing display of quartz laced with thick veins of gold.

"How far does this go?" Eden finally found her senses enough to ask.

"We don't rightly know," Tom replied. "From what my uncle told Aunt Ruth, it most likely goes all the way to China."

"But the worrisome thing is," Ella added, "if someone dug far enough back into the bluffs, they'd come across it for sure."

"It's a wonder no one found it when we had our own 'gold strike'" Sam observed.

"Couldn't 'a happened," Tom said in his usual clipped manner. "This vein runs back from here, not forward."

"At least that's what you *think*. I still think you took one hell of a chance salting the place, like you did," Billy grumbled.

"I knew exactly what I was doing. And, if I recall rightly, you were right there with me tossing those nuggets around."

"But I don't get it." Sam rose to his feet to address

both men. "If you knew about this, and you were worried about the gold being found, why take the chance of letting some overzealous teen-ager find this treasure? It seems like you took an awful big chance just for the fun of watching the whole town succumb to gold fever."

"Oh, I'll admit it was a gamble, but not all that big 'a one. And, from where I stood, if it all worked out like I hoped it would, the risk would pay off two-fold. And, by the way, it did work out like I wanted." The expression on Tom's face was decidedly smug.

"You see, I figured we needed another gold rush—one that would peter itself out, just like the first one. Just the thought of gold sets a person's blood to racing, sort 'a casts a special glow on a place. I figured we needed a little gold fever magic—but not *too* much.

"By putting out those nuggets, we let the fine citizens of Gold Bluff know the thrill of the hunt and we got the new amphitheater dug all at the same time. And all without having to pay a single dollar out for labor."

"Why, you old conniver!" Eden laughed. "So that's why you chose that spot to throw the nuggets. It was all a scheme to get the amphitheater built faster."

"You got it! And it worked too!" Slapping his knee in glee, the old man laughed heartily until a fit of coughing forced him to stop.

"Now you know what an old schemer I've been married to all these years." Ella's words were scolding, but merriment glittered from her twinkling eyes.

Chapter Sixteen

Nine o'clock on a late winter Wednesday night was not a particularly good time for business at the High Trails Café. Which, from Sam's perspective, made it just about perfect. He and Eden needed to talk and they needed to do it without interruptions.

He'd considered and rejected the idea of stopping at either his or Eden's place. They needed privacy, but not *that* much privacy! His hormones had a way of taking on a life of their own whenever he was behind closed doors with the very sexy Ms. McKenna, but this was not the time to indulge those whims.

"There you go, Sammy," Owen, the late evening manager, said as he placed a cup of coffee before each of them. "Give me a holler if you need anything else. I'll be back in the kitchen cleaning up, so if you want a refill just go ahead and help yourselves." Both Eden and Sam remained silent as they watched the rotund middle-aged man amble away from their table.

"Sam, what are we going to do?" Eden asked softly, yet urgently.

"I don't think there's anything we *can* do, except to go ahead and let Tom and Ella deed the land over to us."

"Gee, I don't know. Do you realize the responsibility that would put both of us under?"

"Yeah, I do. And the way I see it, we don't have any choice but to accept it."

"But Sam…"

"No, I mean it, Eden. We've got to do it, no matter how much neither one of us wants it."

"I don't see why they didn't just give it to you. For heaven's sake, they hardly know me."

Sam's sudden bark of laughter echoed throughout the nearly empty restaurant. "But they *do* know me! That's why they want you in on this—to keep an eye on me."

"Oh, I hardly think that's true."

"Oh, it's true, all right. Eden, honey," he reached out to take both of her hands in his own, "before I knew you there's no way on earth I could have been trusted with something like this. Knowing you has changed me for the better, thankfully."

He lowered his gaze to Eden's hands that rested lightly within his own. Cradling them gently in his palms, he let his thumbs stroke the tender flesh. He marveled at their beauty, the creaminess of the skin, the gracefulness of the long tapered fingers. He loved touching them. Heck, who was he kidding? He loved touching every part of Eden. He loved...

"Oh, my God, I really do love her. This isn't just some crazy phase I'm going through. This is the real thing! There's not a cell in my body that is not in love with this woman!"

The realization hit him like a rock, shocking him out of his trance. Having a bucket full of ice dropped on his head would not have begun to equate to the shock that threatened to rock his universe. Sam Gorton in *that* kind of love? In a not-just-for-now, but a forever kind of love? Was it even possible?

"Sam?" Eden's soft voice coaxed him out of his trance. "What's wrong? You look like you just saw a ghost."

"Huh? No! I mean... Where were we anyway?"

"I was saying that I don't feel right about Tom and Ella entrusting me with such an important secret, let alone putting my name along with yours on the deed to the land."

"But don't you see? By giving the gold mine to both of us, we're far more likely to keep the secret safe than if they gave it to just one of us."

"But who's to say I won't move away from Gold Bluff one day? What would you do about the mine then?"

"You're not going anywhere, Eden. I mean... that

is… we need you here…all of us…"

"Sam Gorton! If I didn't know you better, I'd say you were blushing. You aren't coming down with a fever are you?" She leaned across the table to put a hand up to his forehead. "You feel okay, but you sure are acting funny. Are you sure you're feeling all right?"

"I'm fine," he replied, though he wasn't all that sure himself. He felt a trickle of sweat run down his back and wondered why Owen had the thermostat turned up so high.

"Sweetheart, do you have any idea how rich that mine could be?"

She shook her head silently in the negative.

"Well, I'm no geology expert, but I think we may have just seen one of the biggest veins of gold ever found in the entire state of California. Of course, there's no way of knowing for sure how far down it goes without a lot of excavating, but the possibilities are mind boggling!"

"Even without knowing for certain how much gold is down there, we do know what it did to Tom's uncle. It destroyed him."

"Just like it would destroy Gold Bluff if the story ever leaked out."

"But do you think it's right to keep such an important find a secret?"

"You're damn right I do. From the way I see it the world can get along just fine without more gold. Too much money corrupts. No, we have to do what Tom asked us…we've got to keep his secret."

Sam didn't want to waste time thinking about gold. After all, it was just metal—cold, useless metal. No, what he wanted to think about was Eden. Now there was something worth more than all the gold in Fort Knox.

"Sam, you're doing it again," Eden admonished him.

"I'm doing what?"

"You're looking funny, like you're off in another

world."

He didn't say a word, just sat looking at her as if he couldn't get enough of her. He knew he was wearing a goofy grin on his face, but didn't seem to have the power to wipe it away.

"Sam?"

He was right there, ready to tell her everything. The way he felt when he looked into her eyes. The way her smile made his insides melt. The way his heart skipped a beat each time he heard her speak. The way…

But he couldn't do it. Not yet, anyway.

Damn it! What was wrong with him? He couldn't remember ever having problems talking to girls. Far from it, actually. From the time he'd first begun noticing girls, flirting had always come easy to him. *He* was the guy his friends looked up to when it came to romancing the ladies.

It had all been a game to him back then. Oh, he hadn't been one of those guys who kept a record of how many girls he'd won. But he had also never let himself completely lose himself in a woman either. At least not until now. Now his whole future was on the line.

No, that wasn't right either. It wasn't just *his* future anymore, was it? The sudden realization that what he did and said from this point forward could determine not only *his* happiness, but also the happiness of the most wonderful woman ever created scared him senseless.

The stakes were too high for him to take a chance of messing things up. Something as serious as this needed to be approached carefully, with perfect timing. If he blurted out his feelings right now, like he was tempted to do, he risked scaring her off for good. No, he'd better play it cool…let her get used to having him around all the time…*then*, when he was certain she was ready for it, hopefully, he would have found the perfect way to propose to her.

*****

Sam gave Eden a very chaste goodnight kiss outside her front door that night—too chaste, as far as Eden was concerned. Something was wrong with him, but she couldn't figure out what it could be. Had she said something to offend him? Had the responsibility that had been so unexpectedly thrust upon them upset him more than she'd realized?

She sighed as she locked the door for the night then turned to face her empty house. For the first time since moving there she felt lonely. She turned back to the door, intending to unlock it, pull it open, and call out to Sam, calling him back to her arms. But she didn't do it. Begging a man to be with her was not Eden's way. Sometimes she wished she could let her hair down and just let her emotions run wild.

Sighing deeply, she turned to the darkness of her bedroom.

Something had changed between them, but what, she wondered as she lay alone in the darkness. Everything had been going along just fine when all of a sudden he began looking and acting so strange. She thought back over the time they'd spent in the café, remembering each word spoken, each expression on his face. He'd been so normal...so Sam.

But then he'd taken her hands into his and something happened. She recalled the moment with perfect clarity. Cradling her hands in his own, he'd stared at them like they were two alien objects—gazing at them until she thought there was something wrong with them.

From that moment on nothing had been the same. Her sweet, sexy Sam had somehow morphed into a withdrawn, tongue-tied stranger. Darn it! She wanted the old Sam back. The brash, the funny, the tender Sammy she'd come to care for so much.

Chapter Seventeen

Eden remembered reading somewhere that a person could only feel pain on one part of their body at a time—that if you stubbed your toe you would, for the moment anyway, not notice that your head was aching, or whatever other part of your body had been giving you grief. The same could be said, she decided, for life in general. With the play only one week away, she barely had time to think of anything else. The gold mine slipped into the back recesses of her consciousness, along with the odd way Sam had been acting lately. Neither subject was ever too far from her thoughts, yet the myriad of crises relating to the opening of the play usually managed to push them into a corner of her brain where they waited somewhat impatiently for her to acknowledge them.

The thing about Sam was that although he was almost always nearby, helping out wherever and whenever he could, he somehow managed to remain apart from her. In the past he had become something of a fixture at her side. Now he was there, yet never *quite* there. If someone needed help setting up the sound system, there was Sam. Need something painted? Just ask Sam! No task seemed petty to Sam, no person's needs less worthy than another's. He was always nearby helping her students and the other volunteers. Yet he rarely spoke to Eden.

At first she had been so busy getting ready for the play she barely noticed Sam's seemingly lack of interest in being with her. It was a good thing, she told herself the first time she took note that Sam had spent the entire day working all around her yet had barely spoken one word to her. She didn't have time for him right now, she reminded herself as she felt her heart take a dive when he left for the day without so much as a wave in her direction. She told herself she was pleased he was being considerate by not trying to distract her from her duties.

She was overwhelmingly grateful for his help, just as she was for the efforts of all the volunteers. If it wasn't for their efforts the play would never be able to open on time. There was so much work to be done she wondered about her sanity in ever suggesting such an undertaking. There was certainly too much to do for her to waste energy worrying about Sam's seemingly lack of interest. Just the same...

The casting of the play, a hotly contended matter, had been accomplished several weeks before. Costumes had been made, dialogue memorized—well, almost memorized—and sets constructed. When Eden had stopped by the amphitheater yesterday, she was gratified to see that the audience would indeed have somewhere to sit and that the last touches to the stage were nearly complete. The tangy scent of freshly cut lumber and varnish hung pleasantly in the air.

She'd stood there watching all the commotion as woodshop students put the finishing touches on their project. Never in her wildest imagination could she have ever believed all this could have come from her idea of having her students combine their English and history studies by researching the local lore.

Somewhere along the way the project had taken on a life of its own, growing and building until this beautiful structure had been created. And now, in just a few short days the first ever "Gold Bluff—A Living History" would be performed on this very stage.

But just as she was about to give herself a hearty pat on the back for being the one who was behind it all, she was reminded that more than likely she had been nothing more than a pawn on Tom Wenton's game board. Oh, she might have come up with the idea for the play, but from that point on the old man had been the one in control. Clever man that Tom Wenton, clever enough to use her idea to protect his secret for years to come.

She felt a smile creep across her face as she gazed appreciatively at the location of the shell shaped structure. Butted up against the bluffs, it would prevent for all times any future geological explorations from this perspective.

She couldn't resist a small chuckle when she recalled the recent "gold rush" precipitated by the nuggets that had been found during the excavation. What could be a better way to get the amphitheater excavated? And, how better to renew interest in the town's early days then to stage a modern day gold stampede?

She had no doubt that he loved this place and would do just about anything to make the town a success. And she understood he needed a way to keep the story of the hidden gold mine a secret. What better way could there be than to instigate another gold rush that would quickly peter out? They'd found the gold, they'd dug furiously looking for more, experiencing that elusive hope that had kept all the gold miners who had come before them going, only to come to the conclusion that there was no more.

From her prospective as a history teacher, she couldn't be more pleased with the results of Tom's chicanery. What a great history lesson it had been! How better could she have taught her students about the great California gold rush than to let them feel the charge of expectation when they'd learned of the latest strike? To experience the drudgery of digging for hours in the hard packed earth, then hauling buckets of dirt to a nearby stream, standing in the freezing waters where they swirled the contents of their gold pans as they gazed expectantly into the black remains? And then, seeing the glimmer of gold sparkling back at them! Because of Tom Wenton, Eden's students had "seen the elephant."

She let her mind shift into a forward mode, picturing future students doing similar exercises. She could stage yearly gold rushes for her students. And wouldn't it be great to take each new senior class out to the old Wenton homestead for a weekend to let them see firsthand how the local pioneers had actually lived? What a great way to teach history!

Her mind began to race ahead of itself as she excitedly contemplated the coming years. This was how history should be taught, she thought as she recalled the frustrating years she'd spent in the city, trying to engage young minds in their past when history was the last thing they were interested in.

But here in Gold Bluff things were different. It was slower paced…more real. Finally, she would be able to teach the way she'd always wanted to.

Chapter Eighteen

"All right, everybody, let's settle down," Eden called out, elevating her voice so that it would carry to the far edges of the amphitheater. "Now, remember, this is our final dress rehearsal, so no matter what happens, just keep on going. If you forget a word, fake it. Since I don't believe in prompters, you'll be on your own from the moment the curtain rises to the last line of the play.

"Everybody ready?" She paused for a moment, listening for the last bit of restlessness to subside before saying, "All right then, lights down…and…curtain up."

The lights dimmed slowly, filling the amphitheater with darkness. As the last remnants of light disappeared the heavens above put on a show of their own. It was a clear moonless spring evening, with a magnificent show of stars twinkling above.

The silence that settled around Eden was so profound it was as if the whole world was holding its breath. Then, to the right of the stage came the gentle strumming of an acoustical guitar. As the young musician continued strumming his guitar, he was suddenly illuminated by a muted spotlight. The light gained power as he plucked the strings harder, then harder still. Walking up to a microphone that had been placed at the far right of the stage, he began singing the play's narration. The clear strains of George Benson's voice sent a thrill of excitement racing down Eden's spine.

At least she'd thought the rush of excitement she'd felt came from hearing the boy's perfect rendition of the song he and his best friend had written expressly for the play. That was until she realized she no longer stood alone at the foot of the stage. It took only the tiniest breeze carrying Sam's favorite shaving lotion, to let her know he stood nearby. She wasn't sure if the tingling sensation she was now experiencing was because she was happy to have him near, or irritated with him for taking her attention away from the play. Given the current state of her emotions, she could have made a case either way.

"I told you the kid was good." His whispered words came from directly behind her.

"Shhh," she hissed. Then, turning to him, she whispered, "What are you doing here, anyway? I'd think you'd have more important ways to spend your time than watching our dress rehearsal."

"Nope," he grinned as he whispered back. "But don't pay any attention to me. I'm just here to offer moral support. Pretend I'm not even here."

"But..."

"Shhh," he hissed back at her as he pointed to the stage, reminding her where her attention should be directed.

Of all the nerve, she thought as she forced her attention back to the stage. *Who the hell does he think he is, telling me how to do my job? Since when did I need him to remind me what my duties are! He's...he's...*

He's distracting me, that's what he's doing, damn him anyway, she finally admitted to herself. As long as he was within kissing distance her mind would most definitely not be on her work. He'd been so good about staying away from her for so long...why did he have to go and change the rules of the game now, when she needed her concentration level to be at its highest?

"Go away!" she hissed. She turned her head away from the stage just far enough for her whispered words to be heard over her shoulder, but not so far that she lost sight of her students.

He was nowhere in sight. What the...?

She was suddenly aware of the clapping of the few parents and friends who had come to watch the dress rehearsal. The glare of footlights turned to their brightest intensity took her by complete surprise. To her dismay the entire cast of the play was crowding to the edge of the stage, all waiting for her reaction. The play was over? It couldn't be! When had…? Where…?

"So how was it, Ms. McKenna?" several of her students called out to her. "Did we do okay?"

She felt the blood rise to her face as she realized that from the moment Sam left she had not heard one word of dialogue. Her thoughts, rather than being on the stage where they belonged, had been on Sam Gorton. Damn him, anyway! What was she going to do now?

"Why don't you tell me how *you* thought it went? I'm always telling you kids what I think. This time I'd like to hear your own critiques."

It was a total cop out, but she couldn't think of any other way to save the day. Thank heavens she had a great group of students, she thought as one by one they gave their comments and creative suggestions. When it appeared they had all had their say, Eden turned to the small audience, asking them if they had anything to contribute. She was gratified to note that the criticisms from the onlookers were minor. Apparently the play had gone well, even without her full attention.

Full? Who was she kidding? For all practical purposes, she might as well have stayed home.

This wasn't good, not good at all. She'd allowed herself to become so preoccupied by Sam everything else, even her wonderful students, faded by comparison. She couldn't go on like this. She had to do something, and she had to do it soon.

It was a beautiful night, cool yet still pleasant. With the nearly full moon now more than three quarters risen there was more than enough light for her to feel comfortable walking the mile from the amphitheater to her home. Normally she savored every step along the path, enjoying the scent from the cedars and pines that flourished along the way, listening to the river flowing by. But tonight she might just as well have been walking on the moon for all the attention she gave her surroundings.

Barely realizing she had walked so far, she found herself climbing steps and reaching into her purse for her house key. It wasn't until she tried to put the key in the lock, only to find it would not fit, that she realized she hadn't gone to her own home at all. Instead, she found herself standing on Sam's porch. Startled by what she had done, she turned to leave. But then, with more resolve than she believed she possessed, she rapped gently on the door.

The house was still, without even a glimmer of light showing through the etched glass front door. *I'm a complete idiot,* she thought as she stood there in the dark. *But a stubborn idiot,* was her next thought as she knocked once again, this time with more force.

The sudden appearance of light behind the door's glass pane started her heart beating like a trip hammer. With the light came the sure knowledge that she was about to make a complete fool of herself…again.

"Eden? Is that you, honey? What's wrong?"

There he stood, framed by the light from behind, looking like a freshly awakened Adonis. Bare to the waist, the top button of his jeans unfastened, his hair sleep tousled, he was the best looking thing she had ever laid her eyes on.

"I, uh, that is…"

"Here, baby, come on in. We can't have the neighbors seeing you out here this time of night. Think what it would do to your reputation." He pulled her gently but firmly through the door, closing it quickly behind her.

"Sam, I…"

"Honey, look at you, you're shaking like a leaf. Did you catch a chill? Are you feeling all right?"

"I'm fine, Sam, it's just that…"

"Coffee! Let me make you some coffee to warm you up. Or would you rather have a hot cup of tea?"

She reached out to stop him as he turned to go into

the kitchen. "Sam, I didn't come here for coffee...or for tea. I came here because..." Why the heck *had* she come?

"Yes?" he asked as he gently lifted her chin, forcing her to look directly into his eyes. He captured her gaze, mesmerizing her with his gorgeous blue eyes. Her lips parted as if to speak, but the words did not come.

"I...I..." she finally stammered, her eyes still locked on his.

"Yes?" he asked again as he slowly lowered his face toward hers.

"Yes," she sighed as he gently captured her mouth with his.

The kiss was glorious, sweeping away every other thought in her head. Warm, liquid sensations seeped throughout her body as he held her closer, then closer still. Just as the last remnants of reality began to slip from her consciousness she managed to pull herself out of her trance. She stepped out of his embrace, keeping him a safe distance away from her by bracing her hands against his shoulders. Putting a gentle but firm pressure against his shoulders as he tried to pull her close, she frowned up into his eyes.

"Just what sort of game have you been playing lately, Sam Gorton? From the way you've been acting the last couple of weeks I figured you'd lost interest in...this."

"This? What's 'this'?"

"Damn it, Sammy, you know what I mean. First you couldn't seem to get enough of me then all of a sudden you started acting like you hardly know me. Now, here you are again, kissing me like the sun's not coming up tomorrow. What's going on?"

"Like the sun's not coming up?"

"Oh, you know what I mean. The way you kissed me right then, it was like...like..."

"Like I was hopelessly in love with you?"

"Well...maybe something like that." She felt the

heat rising to her face. This was becoming very awkward. What if he told her he'd just been having a little fun with her? That she shouldn't take life so seriously.

"Oh, it wasn't 'something like that', it was *exactly* like that," he said as he pulled her back into his embrace.

"Hopelessly?" Eden whispered as he lowered his lips to hers.

"Hopelessly," was the last word he spoke before he claimed her lips again.

This time it was Sam who broke away. Taking a step back from her, he drew in a deep breath, held it a moment then let it out slowly.

"I'm taking you home right now," he said as he reached for the shirt he had tossed over the back of his dining room chair earlier in the evening. "Where the heck did I put my loafers?" he mumbled as his gaze scanned the living/dining room area.

"But..."

"No, I know what you're going to say...that you don't want to go...and I don't *want* you to go, but it's what we have to do."

"Sam, I don't..."

"Eden, honey, think about it. If we keep on doing what we were almost for sure *going* to do..."

The heat in Eden's face raised another couple of degrees as her very active imagination took her to where he was leading.

"It wouldn't be right, sweetheart. We have your reputation to think about."

"I hardly think..."

"No, we're going to do this thing right...no more sleeping together until *after* the wedding."

"Sam Gorton, is there a proposal somewhere in there? Because if there is, I seem to have missed it." She couldn't keep the grin off her face.

"Proposal...right! We need to do this by the book,

don't we? Wait here just a second, okay?" Completely bemused by his actions, she watched him as he raced across the room to the front door, opened it, stepped through then turned back to her. "Don't go away," was the last thing he said before closing the door.

He returned a few moments later, holding a long stemmed, deep red rose in his hand. Dropping down to one knee before her he offered up the rose as he asked, "Eden McKenna, will you do me the honor of becoming my wife?"

Tears sprang to her eyes as she reached out for his offering. Smiling through her tears she replied, "Sam Gorton, I can't imagine marrying anyone but you."

Chapter Nineteen

This Fourth of July celebration would be like none other in Gold Bluff's brief history. By 10:00 a.m. every household in town was up and moving, busily preparing for the festivities.

Members of the Chamber of Commerce had begun congregating at Founder's Park as early as 7:00 a.m. It was their duty to decorate for the dual celebrations they would be celebrated that day. The first of which, the community wide barbecue, would begin at eleven. At 8:00 a.m. panic hit when the organizers realized there could not possibly be enough picnic tables to accommodate the expected guests.

The Fourth had always been celebrated in Gold Bluff in proper style, garnering very respectable crowds, especially for the evening's fireworks display. But a wedding of two of the town's most prominent residents had never been a part of the festivities before. An informal tally of expected guests revealed that virtually every citizen in town planned on being part of the gala affair.

Mary Jordan, the waitress from the High Trails Café settled jangled nerves when she arrived at a quarter 'till nine and declared that the number of tables would be more than adequate. "People never sit down to eat all at the same time at picnics!" she'd declared, waving away any worries with a flip of her hand. "They come and go…come and go. Now, come on, someone help me cover the tables with this paper I got from the General Store's meat department. Has Sadie gotten here with the flowers yet?"

"She was here about twenty minutes ago, but left when she realized she needed more greenery. Right about now I suspect that every bush in town is in danger of being denuded," Ed Pettigrew remarked with a wry grin.

And so it went, everyone doing all they could to make the day one that no one in town would ever forget.

*****

It would definitely be one Sam Gorton would never forget. Gazing at his image as he carefully drew his razor through thick lather his heart raced with the fear that no matter how careful he was there was no way he was going to get through the operation without nicking the heck out of himself. That was all he needed, to face his beautiful bride as they recited their vows with a face dotted with tiny bits of tissue paper.

They'd written their own vows…which, of course, he could not for the life of him remember. He felt his stomach drop to his knees when he realized that not only had he forgotten the words he had worked so hard to prepare, but he was now absolutely certain he wouldn't even remember her name!

Plunging his face in cold water to wash away the last remnants of lather, he gazed once again at his image and was very relieved to note that not one drop of blood marred his flesh. Taking in a deep breath, he held it for a moment then let it out slowly, feeling himself bask in relief.

It was going to be all right. Nothing could possibly go wrong. Everything was great. This was going to be the happiest day in his life.

*****

Eden was sitting in one of Cut to the Chase's two beauty shop chairs facing the mirror as Ellen Summers carefully wrapped Eden's hair in oversized rollers. After much discussion with the stylist, the two had decided on a soft look for the bride. Eden's long hair would be tamed by the rollers, yet, for the most part, be left to float softly down her back. The sides were to be pulled gently back and fastened at the crown, preventing the hair from obscuring even the slightest bit of her lovely face. The simple style would blend perfectly with the rose crown the bride would wear at her wedding.

Sitting under the drier a few moments later, Eden allowed Ellen to give her a much needed manicure. The nail color she had chosen, "Moon Glow Peach", had a pale opalescence quality that suited Eden perfectly. She watched with satisfaction as the operator applied the second coat of polish, pleased with the mystical effect of the subtle color variations.

She smiled when she thought that before the day was done she would be a married woman. Glancing at the clock on the wall, she realized that in less than four hours she would be Mrs. Sam Gorton.

Eden Gorton. A chill suddenly rushed over her, causing the hand Ellen was working on to shake enough to catch the stylist's attention. Who the heck was Eden Gorton? It sure wasn't anyone *she* knew!

***

By eleven o'clock, all the decorations were in place. The delightful aroma of charcoal fires blended with the fragrance of pine and cedar trees, created an aroma any perfume manufacturer would envy. The ring of horseshoes hitting metal at the horseshoe pits and children's laughter filled the air as games proceeded as planned. A slight breeze played with tree branches, promising to tame the rising summer heat. In other words, it was a perfect day for both a Fourth of July celebration *and* a wedding.

Mary Jordan nodded her satisfaction with the appearance of the decorated tables. She and her crew of helpers had neatly covered each table with white butcher paper, which made a perfect backdrop for bouquets of red roses, and white and blue hydrangeas. Following the same color scheme, Chinese lanterns hung among the trees, each containing tea candles, which Mary was certain would lend a romantic touch to the evening's wedding reception.

Pleased with the results of her efforts, she turned from the picnic area and walked the short distance to the sandy riverside beach. This was where the wedding ceremony would take place, under the white canopy the high school boys were just finishing setting up. She noted with approval the baskets of red and white roses Eden's girl students were waiting to use for the canopy's decorations. Glancing at her watch she decided to offer the girls her assistance. The wedding was only two hours away, which did not leave much time to spare.

By noon, just about everyone in town had arrived. The high school's small brass band belted out a combination of military marches and old time favorites. Beer kegs had been tapped and barrels of iced sodas were at the ready. Sizzling hot dogs were being slapped on buns and passed out to the eager crowd.

A multi-tiered wedding cake held center stage at the head table, which had been placed on a small rise at the outer edge of the other tables. Down the center of the table lay an elaborate braid of ferns and red and white roses. Off to the side of the head table stood another table where guests were invited to sign the wedding book and drop off the gifts they had brought for the happy couple.

"Sammy, come on over here and get yourself a hot dog!" Joe Stanton called over the festive clamor. "And here, let me get you a beer!"

"No, no beer today," Sam declined with a grin. "I don't fancy kissing my new bride with alcohol on my breath," he said as he reached into the soda barrel and drew out an ice cold Coke. "This," he held up the canned drink for Joe to see, "will do me just fine."

"You can at least eat a dog, can't you? Here, let me put some mustard and relish on it. I know just how you like 'em."

Sam eyed the hot dog hungrily, recalling he'd been too wound up earlier in the morning to eat his usual hearty breakfast. Joe had fixed it just the way Sam liked it, loaded with mustard, relish and chopped onions. His stomach growled in anticipation as he reached for the food.

It wasn't until he was raising it to his mouth that he realized the mistake he was about to make. If he wasn't about to drink a beer just before his wedding; what was he thinking even considering eating those onions? And mustard? A picture of himself standing before the judge taking his vows with a huge yellow stain on his pale blue shirt was all it took to make him hand the sandwich back to his friend.

"Better give me a plain dog, just meat on a bun," he said with a rueful grin. "I don't feel like taking any chances with this suit."

*****

"Sweetie, you haven't even touched your lunch. The wedding's only an hour away. If you don't eat something soon you won't have time," Clara Manning reminded the nervous bride.

"Everything looks wonderful, Clara, but I don't think I can eat a bite."

Clara Manning had done herself proud when she'd prepared the pre-wedding luncheon for the bride and her matron-of-honor, Betty Fielding, Sam's secretary. Thrilled to death by the wedding of one of her favorite former guests, Clara had insisted Eden spend her last night as a single woman in the room she had occupied when she first came to Gold Bluff. With Betty staying in the room just across the hall from Eden's, the final preparations for the ceremony had been a breeze.

"Can't you make her eat, Betty?"

Eden gazed at the lovely luncheon her former landlady had so thoughtfully provided. The food was light: crackers and cheese, fresh fruit salad, tomato aspect topped with a dollop of salad dressing and a sprig of fresh mint. But so far all Eden had touched was iced tea, served in tall frosty glasses, also decorated with sprigs of mint.

"For pity's sake, Eden, *eat* something!" Betty chimed in. "If you don't get something in your stomach you're likely to pass out before Judge Elders gets the two of you married! Do you want that to happen?"

"Okay, okay! I'm eating, all right?" she laughed as she popped a square of cheese into her mouth, followed by a crisp multi-seed cracker. "But there's too much here for just the two of us. Why don't you pull up a chair and join us, Clara? There's more than enough for three."

"If that's what it takes," Clara huffed as she reached for a nearby chair. "Then, when we're finished, Betty and I can help you get dressed. Here, give this aspect a taste. It's from a recipe I got from my great aunt."

Promptly at one o'clock, Eden arrived at the picnic site. Mrs. Manning had hired a limousine for the occasion, and was proud to share the spacious interior with the bride and her maid-of-honor, Betty. A cheer of welcome greeted the three women as the driver ushered first Clara, then Betty, and finally the bride out of the car. Sam broke away from the crowd, stepping up to take his bride's hand as he led her down the path to the wedding canopy. The crowd parted as they passed. Closing behind them, they followed the wedding couple down to the riverside.

Soft strains of a string quartet playing baroque tunes drifted up from the riverside, inviting the guests to the wedding. Eden felt as if she were walking on a cloud of happiness as the man she loved led her toward the music, and toward the life they would be sharing from this day forward.

Tom, Ella and Billy were already seated in the first row of folding chairs Eden's students had spent the morning arranging. The two old men considered themselves the match makers who had brought this day about and weren't about to miss a minute of it. For Ella's part, she had come to love both Sam and Eden, taking them to her heart as the children she had never been blessed with. Nothing could have made her happier than the sight of them coming toward her, hand in hand, love radiating from their beautiful faces.

Sam and Eden stood to one side of the altar that had

been decorated with a profusion of white and red roses, waiting patiently for everyone to get settled before stepping over to face the presiding judge. The judge stood at the other side of the canopy as he watched the townspeople settle themselves into their seats.

They look just like statues on top of a wedding cake, Ella thought as she gazed at the bride and groom. Eden had chosen a peasant style soft white cotton dress for the day. The bodice had a wide scooped neck and full, flowing sleeves that were gathered at the wrists. A thin blue ribbon, which matched the shade of her groom's shirt, emphasized her tiny waist. The skirt of the dress, full, with a wide ruffled flounce, came to just above her trim ankles, exposing her thin strapped white sandals.

The wreath of roses took the place of a veil. In her hand she clutched a small bouquet of red roses, completing the color scheme of the day.

When the rustling of the audience settled into an expectant hush, Judge Elders caught Sam's eye then nodded that it was time. The judge and the bridal couple approached the altar, the judge facing the crowd, the couple facing him. Raising his voice to carry over the sound of the river, the judge began the service.

It was a simple, yet moving, ceremony. The words the couple exchanged were their own, more meaningful than those written for them could ever have been. Sam's declaration, "You have changed my life, and for that I will be forever grateful," brought a tear to Eden's eye which slipped unheeded down her cheek. Her own, "I will love you now and forever," gave Sam a rush of relief. Until she said those words he hadn't realized how much he had feared she might get up before the judge and, realizing she was making the mistake of her life, refuse to go on with the wedding.

And then it was over. They'd been declared "man and wife." He had kissed his bride and was receiving congratulations. It was the happiest moment of his life.

"Where will you two live?" Ed Pettigrew asked Sam as the two men shook hands. "That place of yours is great for a bachelor, but I can't see the two of you living there for long."

"We've got that all worked out," Sam replied. "Tom and Ella have given us the greatest wedding present—the perfect lot for a house. The concrete foundation will be poured while we're away on our honeymoon. We should be ready to start building by the time we get back."

Eden waited until the newlyweds were alone before saying, "Sam, I just had a terrible thought. What if the worker's come across the mine while they're grading the lot?"

"Not to worry, Mrs. Gorton. I've got us covered there. Since you were so busy with the wedding plans you probably didn't notice that I've been pretty busy myself the last couple of days. During that time I laid down a foundation for my special gift for you—a gazebo--which, I might add, just happens to cover the opening of the mine."

"A gazebo! What a wonderful idea." Eden couldn't keep from smiling, thinking about what a clever man she had married. What better way to hide the gold mine then to cover it with a heavy layer of concrete? She grinned up at him, picturing the two of them sitting together in the gazebo. Their lives would be filled with the treasure of their love. Who needed more than that?

Both Sam and Eden kissed each of the three old people goodbye after the fireworks display, then allowed themselves to be driven away from the park in the waiting limousine. The old people were tired, but couldn't have enjoyed themselves more.

"Well, I'm glad that's over," Tom said with a sigh. "I don't think I could handle much more of the 'lovey-dovey' stuff."

"Oh, you old poop! You loved every minute of it

and you know it," his wife chided.

"It's nice you gave them the land," Billy interjected, "kind'a kills two birds with one stone, if you know what I mean."

"Now you'll never have to worry about someone finding the gold mine." Ella seemed relieved.

"Yep, that danged gold will be as safe as if it was in Fort Knox," Billy agreed.

"Gold mine? What gold mine?"

"What do you mean what gold mine? You know what gold mine... Oh, no, don't tell me! You weren't just shooting your mouth off again, were you? Don't tell me you've been conning those two youngsters all this time."

Laughing gleefully, Tom slapped his knee. Ella feared her husband would fall off the picnic bench he was laughing so hard.

"Billy, don't let him get to you," Ella said with a frown at her husband. "You know there's a mine. You saw it for yourself more than once. I'll never figure out how you let this old bag of wind get over on you like that."

"I gotcha again, didn't I?" Tom took out an old red bandana to wipe away his tears of laughter.

"Damn you, Tom!"

"You're just too easy.

About the Author:

Maralee Wofford found it easy to describe the beautiful surroundings of her mythical city of Gold Bluff, as she was able to draw extensively from her own experiences of living in Siskiyou County, California's northernmost county. When it came time to people her mythical city, she happily drew upon some of her most treasured memories from her childhood summer vacations spent in Sierra City, CA, a city located in the Sierra Nevada mountain range. Ms. Wofford, writing under the name of Maralee Lowder, is the author of several romance novels and, more recently, three horror books. Not wanting to confuse her readers by this change in genres, she has chosen to write her lighter books as Maralee Wofford. While writing horror books has been a fun change of pace for her, she finds that lighter stories, such as The Gold Bluff Deception, come straight from her heart.

Acknowledgement:

The photo which appears on the cover of this book was taken by the very talented photographer, Janelle Boatright. (JanelleBoatright.com)

If not for a conversation with Laura Pallatin, this book would not have been written. While eating lunch with the author one day she happened to mention hearing about a town that had been designed to echo towns in "the good old days". After the town was completed it they decided that their town needed its own history. So, they wrote one for it. Unfortunately, they came into trouble when the people buying real estate in the town believed they were buying actual historic buildings.

The town of Gold Bluff sprung into the author's imagination that day and became what has been described in The Gold Bluff Deception.

Author's Note:

Although the town of Gold Bluff exists only in the author's imagination, the fact that gold was discovered in the general region where this book takes place is very real. Gold mining, both amateur and professional, is still taking place in Siskiyou County to this day.

Social Media Links:

Facebook: www.facebook.com/MaraleeLowder
Twitter: https://twitter.com/MaraleeLowder
Website: maraleelowder.com/White-Hat.html

Made in the USA
San Bernardino, CA
02 October 2015